DAVID A. ESTES

Ajax
&
Elbow Grease

Cover Design: Sharon Kizziah-Holmes

Paperback-Press
an imprint of A & S Publishing
A & S Holmes, Inc.

ISBN: 1-945669-35-7
ISBN-13: 978-1-945669-35-4

CHAPTER 1

Clara's kitchen

She knew he was over there. She could feel his eyes boring into the back of her head, waiting for her to acknowledge his presence so he could tell her what he wanted her to know.

She didn't need him to tell her. She already knew. It was "that time" again.

Her son John came down from upstairs, all spruced up for a trip to town. Standing at the bottom of the stairs, stretching his patience, John peered past the yellow pine kitchen table to the chipped porcelain sink where his seventy-year-old mother Clara was scrubbing pots and pans with red, work-worn hands. He wished he had a dollar for every time she'd bent over that sink, cleaning up from supper, dishwater-wrinkled fingers clutching a terry cloth rag that outlived its usefulness as a bath towel.

When John was little, Clara told him it took a

lot of Ajax and elbow grease to loosen burnt gravy in the bottom of a skillet. He knew the Ajax was under the sink, but wondered where she kept the elbow grease. Was it good for anything besides getting burnt gravy off the bottom of a skillet? Clara compared scrubbing burnt gravy off the bottom of a skillet to obstacles he'd face in his lifetime.

When John was ten years old he found out what that meant. That was when his father Kyle went to town one day and never came back. John pondered why his father took off without telling him goodbye. He never asked his mother why, and she never told him. The pain of his father's departure was a burden John carried in silence for many years. He finally heard the story from his dying grandmother.

Clara kept scrubbing away at the skillet. A strand of gray hair escaped the rolled up bun on the back of her head. She didn't bother to brush it aside. Unruly hair was at the bottom of her list of things she worried about. At the top of the list was her son John, and that woman who was dragging him down.

Clara grasped the gooseneck handle of the water pump mounted on the cabinet beside the sink. She held the skillet under the spout, gave the handle a couple of furious pumps, and watched the soapy dishwater gurgle down the drain.

She put the skillet aside and went to work on the knives and forks. There weren't many of them anymore. Nobody left but her and John since her ninety-two-year-old father died of emphysema. Seventy five years of inhaling cigarette smoke charred his lungs until there was no room left for breath. She warned John the same thing could happen to him if he didn't give up the filthy habit. The pack of Camels in his shirt pocket looked like it grew there. John didn't smoke till he joined the army, but he kept a fog going much of the time since he came home. She guessed whatever happened in the army caused people to do strange things, like smoking cigarettes and drinking beer.

Clara fingered a tear from her cheek, recalling how she watched her father fade away from inhaling foul smelling cigarette smoke. With a sad shake of her gray head, she mused that somebody was always dying. Just last week they laid Lancie Fleming to rest, rest her soul, after years of pain that nobody found a cure for. Doc Sloan gave up on it, pleading defeat at the end of his medical rope. The week before that, Howie Bolt was gored by a bull he was trying to stick a needle into, and they buried Howie.

Who'd be next? Maybe Simon Colby. Simon was old and fat. He had so many things wrong with him, Doc Sloan wished for someplace else to go when he saw Simon coming.

Or maybe she'd be next, Clara thought with a wry smile. She never spent a day in a hospital, and gave birth to John in her own bed. Unlike most people her age, she suffered from no serious ailments and took no medication. Doc Sloan, after an infrequent check-up last year when she wrestled with that hacking cough she'd fought for "Lord only knows how long," told her she was as "healthy as a twenty-year-old." She allowed herself a smug smile as she reflected that Doc never said which twenty-year-old she was as healthy as. He could have been comparing her to a cat. She had one of those going on twenty-one.

Healthy as she was, for Clara it was not a happy time. There wasn't much to look forward to anymore, except heat, high winds and dust. Why, she looked back on times in the thirties when dust storms turned western Oklahoma midnight dark at high noon. Folks walking home from church looked like chocolate statues by the time they got there.

That was when President Roosevelt tried to save the country by closing the banks and telling farmers to kill their pigs so pork prices would go up. Crops went to hell for lack of rain, and many farmers gave up, sold out, and headed west. Some of them yo-yoed back and forth between Oklahoma and California, unable to make up their minds where they were better off. She heard that Joad bunch had made it out there and never came back. There was a lot of work in California, they said.

People kept trying to convince themselves California was the place to be, with no notion what they'd find when they got there. They were hell-bent on going anyhow. The land of milk and honey, California was. Most of those who went came slinking back, broke, no jobs, no milk, and no honey. Still not believing they were as well off in Oklahoma as in California, some of the die-hards trudged back out there. Like that bird that stabbed itself to death because it couldn't stay away from the thorn tree, they had to go try California one more time.

Clara wasn't ignoring her son. She just had

nothing to say to him right then, and wasn't anxious to get around to what he wanted to talk about. She knew what was pulling at him, and there was nothing she could do to change it.

She was still going on to herself about those fools who bounced back and forth between Oklahoma and California. She congratulated herself that she and John stayed put. Life in Oklahoma wasn't all peaches and cream, but at least they had a roof over their heads and food on the table, which most of those people didn't find out west. She was so busy thinking about it she hardly heard John's husky-voiced announcement.

"I'm going into town."

That wasn't news. Clara had heard it numerous times before since John's wife, that little snip of a Holly, walked out on him.

Holly and Clara's husband Kyle were cut from the same cloth. Holly just up and took off one day and nobody heard from her either. Not so much as a note, nor a phone call. Nothing.

Clara didn't care. She couldn't care less if she never heard from Holly again. She knew John wasn't over it though. Probably his excuse for spending so much time with that bitch in Blessing.

Her stubby fingers kept scrubbing away at the dirty dishes. She knew she couldn't talk John out of what he had in mind. He was thirty-eight-years old. He didn't have to ask anybody if it was all right to do whatever he wanted. Except for selling the farm to that hog outfit, which he couldn't do because it didn't belong to him. It belonged to her. It fell to her when Kyle took off, and nobody could do anything about it unless she said so.

"Going into town" was a pure and simple pronouncement of her son's intentions. The fire in his belly didn't strike often, but when it did, it stubbornized him so he had to find a way to put it out. Pain pills wouldn't have solved the problem. It was an itch scratching couldn't fix. And he couldn't drink enough beer at the Welcome Back Bar and Grill to put out the fire. The solution was not the one Clara preferred, but she resigned herself to the sad fact that she didn't have a vote. John made up his mind he was going into town, and into town he would go. Wild horses couldn't block the trail.

Clara was well aware it wasn't just "into town" her son was going. She knew he was going to see that woman he couldn't get enough of after Holly left. It had been going on between him and Josie for a year or two. It started soon after Holly stormed out. John still cared more about Holly than about anything else, including farming. Farming still came in a distant second to the pressure between his legs when the urge struck. Clara lost hope he would ever put farming ahead of anything else. When he came home after Korea he stayed on the farm because she wanted him to, and there was nobody else to do the planting, fertilizing, and harvesting.

John's daddy was a good farmer, but Kyle didn't stay around long enough for John to learn much from him. About everything John knew about working the dirt he learned from his aged grandfather who forgot most of what John needed to know.

Had anyone asked Clara why Kyle left she'd

have said she didn't know. She told herself that story long enough and often enough she started believing it. She always blamed her runaway husband for whatever went wrong on the farm and in their life together. She convinced herself she really didn't know why Kyle went off without telling anybody, leaving her and eight-year-old John without a sniff of goodbye. She guessed she'd never know now. She grudgingly admitted she missed Kyle. He was a good husband, but he had no backbone. Even so, losing hope of seeing him again after all those years, Clara's caring had worn thin, especially now when she had John all to herself since Holly was no longer an obstruction between herself and her son.

John knew why his father left. His grandmother told him, but he didn't let Clara know what she said. He loved his mother, but learning from his grandmother why his father deserted them cast a different light on how he felt about her. Their conversations became strained and less frequent. Clara skirted subjects she'd rather not talk about. And, though she thought little of the change that came over John since he learned of the rift between his mother and father, she accepted John's reticence as a trait of close-mouthed growing boys.

John didn't love the land the way a farmer must to make a go of it. When John went to fight that Asian war a couple of years after high school, Clara knew there was a chance he might not come back. Every day most of what she heard them talk about on the radio and television news was how many boys died in Korea the day before. She didn't draw an easy breath until she saw John walking up the lane toward the house after the war was over. Her father drove her to the Railways Bus station in Blessing two or three times a day, hoping John would be on one of them. He wasn't. Every time she showed up at the bus station and John didn't, Clara was disappointed. She went back to worrying about him all over again.

John was no good at letter writing, so she didn't know when he might be coming home. The happiest day of her life was when she looked out her kitchen window and saw him ambling up the lane with his duffel bag slung over a shoulder. She caught a quick breath with a trembling hand to her mouth, stifling a relieved shout. "Hello, Mama," John said, when he appeared in the back door.

Clara grabbed him in grateful arms, hugged him for a long moment, and cried out loud, thanking God he was safely home.

It didn't take long for John to get restless. Within a week or so, he started thinking about what he was going to do with the rest of his life. In the army he saw places he'd like to see again, and his plans for the future didn't include spending what was left of it on his mother's farm. Even so, he stayed because she needed him. His father gone, grandfather dead, the chores and crops weren't being tended. Clara was right. After he lost Holly, John's interest in the farm faded.

John and Holly Burgard dated in high school, and traded letters occasionally while he was in the war, she more often than he. When he came home, she invited him to her house for dinner "sometime."

He never felt comfortable in the presence of her college professor father, but went because he liked Holly and she asked him to come.

Burgard turned up his supercilious nose at the prospect of his daughter being married to a man "with dirt under his nails, and boots knee-deep in hog shit."

In spite of her father's objections, John and Holly continued seeing each other. A year after John returned from the army, he and Holly stood at the altar of the Blessing Methodist Church and answered "I do" to whatever Preacher Simmons said.

Clara thought after the wedding John would settle into farm life and things would be different. They were. She and Holly never found a way to get along with each other. They spent little time trying to resolve their differences, at each other's throats much of the time. When Holly walked away that day three years ago, the wall that stood between Clara and John came tumbling down. Clara was again in sole possession of her son.

The night after Holly left, John chased all over trying to find her but didn't know where to look.

He spent longer days in the fields to which he felt no closeness, but it gave him a reason to be away from the houseful of memories of Holly. When it got too dark to work the fields, if you wanted to find John Willingham, you looked for him at The Welcome Back Bar & Grill in Blessing, as if he hoped to find in a bottle something to deaden the pain of losing his wife.

Clara got the blame for Holly's leaving, of

course. Oh, John never said anything about it out loud, but she knew by the way he looked at her and the long silences between them, not like before he married Holly.

She and John talked freely then, about whatever was on their minds, with no secrets. Since she left, Holly's name was rarely mentioned, like she never existed—like Holly and John weren't married for nine years before she left. Clara wouldn't admit it, but John knew she was jealous of the time he'd spent with Holly. John didn't like working the farm, but Clara guessed he didn't know how to do much of anything else. Except for how to fight a war, killing people he didn't know, never heard of, and had nothing against, way off over there in some God-forsaken place called Korea.

She blamed Harry Truman for not allowing MacArthur to go ahead and finish the job so her son could come home. A generation of young American men had already soaked the Asian soil with their blood half way around the world in a place they wouldn't want to die. Many of them were shipped home in bags and boxes. Countless numbers of survivors were hardly recognized as the sons and fathers who left home to do the fighting for a country full of people who didn't even know where Korea was, and didn't care what went on there.

Every day Clara thanked God that John came back without a scratch, three years older and twenty-seven pounds heavier than when he left home.

Watching his mother fidget at the sink, John drew a deep breath, like she was stalling for time, hoping he'd go away so she wouldn't have to say what was on her mind, what she'd kept to herself for much too long.

For John, fretting over his mother's ignoring him would be a waste of time. A lifetime of waiting taught him there was no use talking till Clara was ready to listen.

Dishwater dripped from her wrist as she brushed away the errant strand of hair. She wiped her hands on the apron sewed from a Pillsbury flour sack. Puffy cocoons of aging skin below her pale green eyes merged into sunbursts of wrinkles at the corners. Her small ears lay flat against her head, and half a dozen stiff black hairs stuck up from the bridge of her nose. When she smiled, which was seldom anymore, her thin lips revealed a set of false teeth she got when she was twenty-six years old because of infected gums.

Finally she looked around with a solemn nod. She took up a dish towel and began wiping plates, placing them in the cupboard. John thought she was being more careful with the dishes than she needed to be, killing time, probably thinking about some barb she hadn't used for a while to stab him.

"I guess you'll be going to see that Josie woman again," Clara said casually, as if she didn't really care. She paused for his response that didn't come. "Some folks say Josie is a fancy woman."

John knew his mother loved him. He couldn't say why, except that parents were supposed to love their kids, as their kids loved them. It was a given, a built-in, a rule that wasn't written down any place, something that wasn't talked about, a part of living together and loving each other that came naturally, without effort. Still, tolerance of his mother's views of sensitive matters wasn't a characteristic with which John escaped her womb. His backbone stiffened at her bickering and badgering.

It kept him from going out of his mind. The alternative was to walk away, leaving her darting epithets at his departing back.

"What does that mean, Mama?" he said.

"Well, you know," she hedged.

"I know Josie, but I don't know what you mean when you say she's a fancy woman. You make it sound like something dirty."

Josie Cramer was a cross Clara didn't want to carry. She didn't have to guess where John wound up when he went to town. The spinster Parker sisters, across the corner from Josie's yellow bungalow, kept Clara informed of John's comings and goings. Her phone line heated up anytime the sisters saw John on his way to Josie's front door.

Clara stared into the unblinking eyes of her son, scrubbed and slick shaved as always when he went to see "her." John was wearing his best khaki pants, red and black plaid shirt buttoned at the collar, the Justin boots she bought with her egg money for his birthday.

"Some folks say Josie's a whored."

CHAPTER 2

John took another breath to sustain him through the crisis and bit his tongue. A defense against lashing out at her, against shouting what he wanted to say in response to his mother's vindictive accusation, things he kept stored up until he thought he might explode. Things he hoped he would never be angry enough to fling back at her. He kept reminding himself that she was his mother, deserving of her son's respect.

"What do you say, Mama?" he said.

"Some folks say—"

"I don't care about some folks. I want to know what you say."

Clara's heavy, calico-clad body shifted when her eyes did until she looked him squarely in the face. "I think that woman is corrupting you," she said.

"Corrupting me?'

"Corrupting you."

"Well, Mama, I'm thirty-eight years old. I like being with Josie, and she likes being with me. If that's what you call corrupting me, I guess I'll just have to suffer it out." He took a step toward the stairs.

"Are you leaving now?" she asked.

"I'll just get my hat."

Clara knew when John got all duded up it was time for him to "let loose the tiger" that struck his vitals so fiercely he could no longer fight the urge. Sometimes he'd be gone overnight, other times maybe a day or two. And once in a while he wouldn't show up back at the farm for a week.

Clara's old orange tomcat had similar habits. He too sometimes disappeared overnight and came home when he felt like it. She never knew when to expect him either. Often when John came home after a trip to town, he made a beeline for the tool shed, cranked up the old Allis Chalmers tractor, and headed for the field without a word to his mother.

He felt no obligation to explain where he went, with whom, nor what he did while he was gone. But Clara knew, thanks to Josie's nosy neighbors. The Parker sisters derived some vicarious pleasure from reporting to Clara about John's visits to see Josie. The last time they reported, the sisters saw John go into Josie's house at seven o'clock in the evening. They couldn't say whether he ever came out because they had to leave for a circle meeting at the Methodist Church. Five days later the sisters saw John emerge from Josie's front door, but they couldn't say whether he was with Josie the whole time, or if he left, came back, and left again.

For some reason, Clara contrived the notion that John didn't like women. No woman, except for Holly. Since he and Holly split—the reasons for which Clara would rather not talk about—John showed little interest in the opposite sex. But, he hadn't found a way to get along without them either. Without Josie anyhow.

John reappeared at the bottom of the stairs. "A man needs to get away sometimes, Mama," he said.

"You think I don't know that?" she said. "You think I don't have the same urgings you have? Just because I'm old don't mean I'm made of wood. It hurts," she cried, as though blaming her son for the pain. "But there's nothing I can do about my urgings."

John placed an arm across her slumping shoulders, and drew her to him. "All my life," he said, "I've tried to find ways to please you. I came back to the farm after Korea because grandpa broke his hip and couldn't work it any more. You couldn't do it alone, and help was hard to come by.''

You know how your daddy loved this place," she said.

"The land meant something to him, Mama," he said. "Gee and haw meant something to him. Whipping that old team up one furrow and down another was important to him. Sifting dirt through his fingers, planting seeds, watching crops grow. All that meant something to him.

"I've tried, Mama, but the war showed me places better than sweating it out here, scratching a living out of the dirt, praying for rain that doesn't come, on crops that can't make it without it.

"Left to me, I'd sell out to that hog outfit and let them worry about the corn and beans."

"I can't do that, son."

"You've worked hard all your life, Mama. It's time you had some rest. If we sold out, we could go someplace where you wouldn't have to scratch and scrub your life away. Maybe we could go to some of those places we'll never see from this farm."

"You couldn't leave the land, John," she said, as though his leaving would desecrate hallowed ground. "Your daddy sweated blood and tears to pay this place off. He wouldn't want you to ever leave it."

He let her go and turned away. "Don't push, Mama."

They'd been through it all many times before, her pushing, his turning away. He wished he could feel about the land as his father did. Still, stuck in his craw was the question he lived with most of his life.

Where was his father now? The adulation a young boy feels for the father he idolized faded with time, but the question was still there. Why didn't he come home that day, instead of just taking off, telling nobody he was leaving, where he was going, or when he'd be back?

His grandmother's description of why his father went away was etched on his brain, but knowing why didn't help. The questions screamed for answers that never came.

John remembered the sadness in his mother's eyes the day Kyle left. But, after she didn't hear from him for six days, Clara went into a rage. She screamed and swore, back and forth she raged, up and down the stairs, damning Kyle to hell, berating him for leaving them alone. Eight-year-old John ran terrified from the house to the barn, and hovered in the hayloft until he thought the rage had passed and it was safe to come down.

John loved his mother, but sometimes he hated her for what his grandmother told him. Alone in the field, mechanically guiding the tractor up one row and down another, he sometimes hated his father too, but it didn't last. He couldn't deny he longed for his father to come home. The worst times were when Clara went into fits of hysteria, belittling John for causing the agony of bringing him into the world. The burden of guilt his mother's tantrums piled on him he carried with sadness, along with the confused mind of a young boy made to feel responsible for her unhappiness.

"I stayed here because you asked me to," John said to Clara. "I lost my wife because you weren't comfortable with her around."

"It wasn't all my fault," Clara cried.

"No kitchen was big enough for two women, you said."

"Oh, sure," Clara cried, mopping tears on her apron. "Blame your poor old mother for your break-up with that little snip!"

John felt the venom, bearing still the scars of past such encounters. He turned on a heel and headed for the door.

"That's right!" she screamed at his back. "Go spend the night with that little whore and leave your poor old mother all alone. God will punish you for that, you'll see!"

"Mama," John said, "I'm sorry if I hurt you."

"Hurt? You don't know what hurt is! You don't care about me. All you care about is that precious little whore. Go on! Go stick your big old thing in her and make her happy. Don't worry about your mother. My suffering don't matter."

From her twisted lips spewed ugly words John never before heard her utter.

"For nine long months I carried you in my body," she raged, "and the Lord told me you'd be a boy. When that man ran off and left us, I didn't care, because I knew you'd take care of your mama. I knew you would never leave me."

"That man," as John would learn, suffered from years of belittling and denigrating insults from Clara's tongue.

He was twelve years old when his grandmother drew him to her with an aged arm, a mass of colorless, sagging flesh. She pressed his head to her bosom, agonizing with him, sharing the pain of his wrenching sobs.

She related the heart-breaking tale of conflict, the wall of challenge between his mother and father.

"I love you more than I ever loved your mama, John," his grandmother wheezed in her dying moments. "She's my daughter and I love her, but I can't leave this world without telling you the straight of it.

"Your mama ran your daddy off this place. He left because he couldn't put up with it any longer. She was always at him about something till he was half out of his mind.

"Your daddy was a good man, but he was not a strong man. Nothing he did pleased your mama. When he took all he could of her nagging and crabbing and cutting him down, he just up and left. He loved you, John. He'd have taken you with him, but your mama would've killed him before she'd let you go.

"I know it hurts. It has hurt me all this time, watching you suffer, keeping it bottled up, wanting to let it out. I didn't want you to spend the rest of your life wondering what happened, knowing she'd never tell you." With arthritis-twisted fingers she brushed his sandy hair. "Now," she said, "you know the truth of why your daddy went away and never came back."

Hearing the reasons for his father's leaving didn't ease the pain of losing him. The hurt was still there, gnawing at John's insides, and the wound didn't heal. His fondest memories were of learning from his father how to handle a rifle, skin a rabbit, fillet a bass, and drive a tractor when he was seven years old.

Camping in the woods, or on the river bank overnight, was a special treat, even when cold shivers wrinkled the skin on his back at the terrifying sound of a rattler's threat. One thing John didn't learn from his father was how to bear his being gone.

John looked back with sadness to the day his grandmother cried with him, and wondered why he didn't tell his mother what she said, but he could not. "Goodbye, Mama," John said on his way out.

Clara wiped her eyes. "When will I know to look for you back?"

"When you see me coming."

"John."

"Yes, Mama?"

"Don't bring home no more trouble—like that other time."

He pulled the door to behind him as he left

Simon Colby's Sak'n Pak

Six years ago Thelma Colby died of pneumonia. For thirty-eight years, she and Simon operated their little mom-and-pop Sak'n Pak grocery store on the west edge of Blessing. Their son Isaac was killed in that hunting accident the year before Simon lost Thelma, and his two daughters lived with their families half way across the country—one in Colorado, the other in Tennessee. So, left alone at sixty-nine, Simon thought about selling out, or just slapping a lock on the door of the Sak'n Pak and calling it quits.

Bailey Hooper tried to talk Simon into settling near him and his wife where they retired in Sun City, Arizona. Bailey sold his insurance agency after forty-seven years, and had no worries about money. Bailey could live any place he wanted.

After Bailey's wife Elizabeth paid a visit to her sister in Sun City, he bought a home there. Elizabeth said that was where she wanted to die. Eight months later she did.

All Arizona got from Simon was a passing thought. He calculated that he wouldn't get much of anything out there, except twelve months of sunshine, and half of that was hotter than hell had any right to be. He figured Oklahoma would work as well for him as Sun City, and for a lot less money. Simon heard the talk of how wonderful California was, and gnawed on that bone for a day or two as a place to put down new roots. But, at sixty-nine, he didn't have enough roots left to put down in some place he never laid eyes on. What he learned about the hustle and bustle, the high cost of living turned him against California.

He and Clara were two of the few who didn't swallow the California bait years ago. And, for Simon, the prospect of Florida—beautiful beaches, "land of eternal sunshine"—lasted about as long as a snowflake in August. Half of Florida got blown away about every other year, and Simon would bet his Social Security check there wasn't enough of it left to fuss over.

In his early mental meanderings, Simon thought of retirement as a time to settle down with Thelma in one of those little grass shacks in Hawaii where he wouldn't have to do anything but watch other people stumble around on the beaches, digging their toes in the sand, bobbing up and down in the water. Of course, Thelma's passing changed all that. Anyhow, those time wasters were at the bottom of the list of things Simon and Thelma enjoyed doing.

Simon thought he would look pretty silly running around in one of those skinny-dipping swimsuits with his fat middle hanging out. When they traveled, he and Thelma preferred taking country roads instead of the heavily traveled main highways, because she liked browsing through the small town flea markets and visiting historical sites. In the end, Simon knew the best place for him was where he was born and raised—right there in Blessing, Oklahoma. Even with its shortage of sophisticated attributes like Walmart and McDonald's, Thelma would want him to stay put, and put was where he stayed.

After Danny Rankin opened his big super store on the Blessing square, Simon's little Sak 'n Pak neighborhood market was still more convenient for long-time customers to swing by and pick up a gallon of Johnson's Dairy milk, or a loaf of Butternut bread.

And Simon's was still a favorite stop for morning coffee. Anybody who bought something was entitled to a free cup, and the pot was always hot on the Franklin stove.

In years past, Simon provided groceries for families who fell on hard times. Out of his pocket he also paid doctor bills, bought coats and shoes in the winter for kids whose parents had no money to pay for them. Most of those who benefited from Simon's generosity didn't forget what he did for them when they needed help. They paid him back when they got on their feet, some only a few dollars a week until the slate was clean.

Mayor Skelly Wilks took advantage of Simon's generosity. Skelly was a miserly parasite who didn't feel the need to buy anything to qualify for Simon's free coffee. Skelly's mindset was, as mayor of the town, he was entitled to every sip of Simon's sweetened coffee, and paid for none of it.

The mayor was about as welcome at the Sak'n Pak as the ingrown toenail Si had Doc Sloan cut out last fall. The mayor nagged at Simon to "write off and forgive" the sixty-eight-dollar coffee debt he piled up over the years. Simon would do it for anybody, except the tight-fisted mayor.

"Just put it on my tab," Skelly said, sending Simon into an attack of silent exasperation.

Even so, Simon added it to the niggardly mayor's tab, which Skelly never paid. Skelly went through some difficult times with his wife Beulah before she died of cancer, and Simon took it easy on the bereaved mayor. But that was a long time ago. Beulah was Thelma's friend, else Simon would have cut Skelly off without a sip. Simon once snorted to John Willingham that Skelly was elected mayor because he was the only man in town who wasn't working.

Skelly's job as mayor paid him a yearly salary that amounted to less than the Yankees paid Mickey Mantle every time he swung the bat. In addition to his job as mayor, Skelly took to driving a milk truck for the local cheese plant, and could well afford to pay his way. Even so, Skelly exercised what he believed to be his mayorship's privilege of not paying for his consumption of Simon's coffee.

Simon was not hard up for money, but he decided enough was enough, and it was time he settled the score with the mayor. "Tight as a trailer hitch, and nosier than a chicken-sniffing fox," Simon grumbled.

Skelly Wilks was the community repository for useless information. He'd tell everything he knew to anybody who'd listen, and knew nothing, except what somebody told him.

Now, Simon learned Skelly was spreading a tale about the resurrection of Hamp Hargrove, and Simon would put up with the mayor for long enough to find out what it was.

Skelly's faded blue 1939 Dodge pulled up and parked in front of the Sak 'n Pak.

Simon knew the mayor would come in to mooch another cup of coffee. When he came through the door, Simon was ready.

"What the hell is this crap you're spreading around about Hamp Hargrove being alive?" Simon said.

Skelly was in no hurry with his answer. He poured himself a cup of coffee from the pot on Simon's stove. He wrapped his bony fingers around the tin cup and sipped at it. He wiped his mouth with the back of his hand, squinted at Simon, and looked for some sign that would tell him how much the storekeeper was in a frame of mind to put up with.

"What's that you say?" Skelly said.

Simon's appraisal of Skelly was that he was born about a quart and a half shy of a gallon, and at fifty-eight his brain still hadn't caught up with the rest of him.

Wiry, squint-eyed and goateed, Skelly took a sip from the cup, savoring the flavor that Simon hoped he would choke on.

Simon said, "What the hell is this crap about Hamp Hargrove being alive?"

"Well now, Si," the mayor whimpered. As an

aside, he said, "Would it be all right if I put a little more sugar in this one?"

Simon held his tongue and waggled his head in what looked to Skelly like yes.

"You know John Willingham," Skelly said, dumping in another spoonful of sugar.

"Hell yes, I know John Willingham! Everybody knows John Willingham!"

"I haul John's milk."

"I know you haul John's milk! You haul everybody's milk!"

"Well, Si, John Willingham told me Hamp Hargrove was out to his place trying to get him to sell out to that hog outfit over in Arkansas."

"Willingham told you that?"

"Sure as hell did."

"And was he damn sure it was Hamp Hargrove he was talking to?"

"Positive ID. I asked him myself. I said, John, are you damn sure it was Hamp Hargrove you was talking to?"

Simon waited for Skelly to tell him what John said, but all he got was a blank stare.

"Well," Simon said, trying not to explode until after he found out what he wanted to know. "What did John say?"

"Sure as hell was."

"Sure as hell was what?" Simon yelled, two degrees short of exploding.

"Sure as hell was Hamp Hargrove."

In a smoldering, silent fit of collapsing patience, Simon stroked his face with an open palm from his freckled forehead to his triple chin. He grabbed up a wet towel and began silently wiping Skelly's coffee drippings off the counter. He tossed the towel aside, and shuffled over to the coffee pot and poured himself a cupful. He draped his bulk over a wooden stool at the counter, and faced the unsuspecting mayor.

"Skelly," Simon said in as calm a voice as he could muster, "how long have you been coming in here mooching coffee off of me?"

"Well, now, let me see," Skelly said, stroking his whiskered chin. "I've been mayor for eleven years, and before that I was—"

"How long, Skelly?" Simon roared.

"It must've been the year my wife Beulah died. Going on nine or ten years."

"Ten years!" Simon seethed, control hanging by a thread. "For ten years you've been parking your skinny ass on my stool, and you never once offered to pay for a cup of that high-priced frog piss you've been gulping down!"

"Well now, Si—"

Simon rose. He pointed to the door. He shouted at Skelly.

"Skelly Wilks, mayor of Blessing, champion skinflint of the State of Oklahoma, get the hell out of my store!"

Skelly threw up his hands, defending himself against what he feared would be blows from the irate storekeeper, attempting a protest that came off sounding more like a whimper.

"Go on," Simon said, "I don't want to see you around here for a while."

The mayor slumped out and climbed into his

aging Dodge, wondering what came over Simon to make him go berserk. The mayor was struck by the unhappy prospect of paying for his coffee at Dixie's Do-Drop Inn across town. Dixie didn't contribute to charity unless someone else paid for it.

Skelly gave his balding head a bewildered shake as the Dodge crawled away like a scolded dog.

Simon slammed the door shut.

His outburst didn't solve anything, but he felt better for it. For years he fought the urge to challenge the mayor about his deadbeat habits, and Skelly's outlandish story about Hargrove being alive gave him a reason to get it done.

Simon watched Seth Gibbs lay Hargrove's mountainous body to rest in the Berean Baptist Church cemetery two years ago.

CHAPTER 3

Much ado about Dude

John's white collie Rascal trotted ten paces ahead of him. Every few seconds, Rascal stopped and looked back to be sure John was still coming.

A couple of years ago, Rascal showed up at John's back door wagging his tail. His long pink tongue was hanging out, and his eyes reflected a sad "feed me" look only a hungry dog can display.

John scratched Rascal's ears and fed him a plateful of table scraps. Rascal licked his hand.

Rascal found a home, and became a permanent resident of the Willingham farm.

When they reached the end of the lane, Rascal paused, twirled his fluffy tail in a windmill motion, lolled his tongue, and listened for John to say, "Wait here." John's best friend stretched out on his belly beside the road, and watched until he walked out of sight, then moseyed back down the lane to the house.

John was mulling over his mother's parting comment about "trouble like that other time", which she wouldn't let him forget.

There wasn't much to it, not nearly as much as Clara enjoyed making of it. All it amounted to was a little scuffle at the Welcome Back Bar & Grill, where some drunk was slapping a woman around.

No man worth his salt would stand around and watch him do it. John didn't either. He stroked the man's chin with a folded fist to protect the woman

The stroke knocked the batterer backward against a table. The woman turned on John, screamed obscenities, and pounded his chest with her fists.

Deputy Limpy Logan wandered into the place, looking lost, as if waiting for someone to tell him where he was.

In the past, Limpy maligned the Welcome Back for the rowdy goings on in "that den of iniquity." It was not a place where he wanted to be caught rubbing elbows with the riff-raff.

Even so, to make it look like he knew what he was supposed to be doing, Limpy made a quick study of what the ruckus was about, surveyed the situation with a jaundiced eye, and reverted to looking lost. He didn't question anybody because he didn't know what to ask; and, after a few minutes of watching people wonder why he was there, Limpy pronounced the mix-up over.

Limpy asked John if he'd like a ride home. John took him up on it, and Limpy dropped him off at the Willingham farm.

John invited him to share a cup of coffee in Clara's kitchen.

Logan crawled out of his pickup and limped inside behind John.

Clara eyed the deputy with suspicion.

She couldn't conjure up a reason to respect the hapless lawman, but brought the pot and poured his cup full anyway.

"Wasn't nothing serious," Limpy said when she asked him what happened. "Just a little mix-up us lawmen run into about every time a new calf drops."

Clara was mortified. She could hardly wait for Limpy to be gone. "Nothing like this ever happened in our family before," she complained to John, once the deputy was out of earshot. "First criminal we ever had!" she said.

It wasn't all bad, John recalled. He got a ride home out of it. Would he do it again? Damn right.

In the army men flew off the handle to relieve tension, frustration, or anger, not knowing what lay ahead for them. Such encounters often led to bare-knuckled fisticuffs, or a wrestling match nobody won.

John Willingham wasn't one of them. He engaged in no such heated activity since grammar school until the Welcome Back incident.

Stroking the man's chin was an instinctive reflex, like rescuing a small child from the path of a runaway train.

Growing up in school, John's friend Billy Gerber was the fighter. Billy fought anybody any time anywhere just for the jolt he got out of it.

When it was over, Billy walked away with his arm around the shoulders of the kid with the bloody nose.

John and Billy served in Korea together.

Billy got shot up in a clash with the swarming Chinese in the Kumwha Valley. He could have gone home, but after months of getting rebuilt at Walter Reed, Billy volunteered for another tour in Korea. Once again he shipped out, rejoining his old outfit in the battle for Pork Chop Ridge. Five weeks later, Billy was cut down by an enemy machine gun he was leading a charge against.

Billy Gerber was the only hero Blessing ever had. If you went to City Hall you'd see the plaque with his picture on it mounted on the wall. Every day until she died at age seventy-three, Billy's mother went to City Hall, kissed the plaque, caressed it with her fingertips, and said a prayer for Billy.

Mayor Wilks complained that Mrs. Gerber's visits "disturbed the City Hall staff," which consisted of himself and Ellie Parks.

Ellie was the unflappable volunteer watcher of the telephone which seldom rang. She was sixty-one years old, a fixture in the mayor's office before Skelly got there. Ellie couldn't care less what the mayor thought about Mrs. Gerber's daily ritual. She let him know in no uncertain terms that she didn't appreciate his insensitive remarks aimed at the mother of the local war hero.

The mayor slunk away with a hurt look on his face.

The recollection brought John back to his

conflict with his mother. His grandmother told him Clara belittled his father until she nearly drove him out of his mind.

John knew what that meant. That was why he stormed out of the house before his latest clash with his mother got worse.

At Josie's he could relax with beers and burgers and escape Clara's fiery outbursts.

Along the lane, John was hardly aware of the fields of tasseled corn lining both sides. Patches of crabgrass struggled toward the high center of the lane, not yet beaten bare by truck and tractor wheels.

The lowering sun cast red and yellow streaks across the Sunday evening sky, as John took off with long strides toward town.

He made the turn onto the road to Blessing before he realized he was on foot.

That was what those episodes with Clara did to him. He couldn't blame her for his mental lapses, but their disagreements were more frequent, mostly because of her obsession with the time he spent with Josie.

Thinking about it made him sad, and suddenly weary. He wished he had driven the Ford pickup parked beside the well house. Or he could have driven that old Pontiac which stood for years in the tool shed. The thought brought half a smile.

Before he died, John's grandfather insisted on driving the Pontiac, referring to it as his "last frontier of independence." John worried that grandpa would kill himself, or somebody else, with his erratic driving. Since grandpa died, the Pontiac was rarely driven.

Clara couldn't drive and showed little interest in learning. John encouraged her learn anyway, for she might need to drive the Pontiac sometime "in case of an emergency," with no thought as to what the emergency might one day be. He stretched his patience and suffered through a couple of training sessions, showing Clara how to start the motor, shift gears, and "stay on your side of the yellow line."

Even with John's instructions, Clara didn't feel confident enough to drive, and didn't sit behind the wheel without him at her side.

The three-mile walk to town was no challenge for John. He'd walked it before, and welcomed the opportunity to cool off and think out some of the nagging pushing itself to the front of his mind.

Like Clara's tangles with Holly on the farm before Holly left. Tension between them hung like fog on the catfish pond up north of the barn.

For twelve years Holly put up with Clara's thinly cloaked insinuations.

One day while John was baling fescue, Clara and Holly got into it over something he'd bet neither of them remembered. But it was serious enough to tell Holly it was time for her to move out and move on.

She was tempted to leave before, but didn't because of John. This time, she bounded up the stairs, threw a few things into a small bag and took off toward Blessing on foot.

With a smug smile, Clara watched her go and slammed the door behind her.

When John came in from the field, Clara told

him Holly was gone.

John suspected his mother shaded the facts in her favor, unable to disguise her pleasure of finally being rid of her saucy daughter-in-law.

As when Holly suffered the two miscarriages, Clara made no attempt to hide her joy that Holly departed the premises.

John cast his mother a disapproving look, pretty certain of how the encounter began and who was at fault. He leaped into the truck and headed for town. With a heavy foot on the gas, he hoped to catch Holly before she got there.

John's first stop was at the Trailways Bus station. He dashed in and asked Susan Dobbs, the ticket agent, if Holly had been there.

Susan told him she saw somebody drop Holly off out front. Holly came inside and bought a ticket.

"Who dropped her off?"

"I didn't see who it was," Susan told him. "I thought it might have been you."

"Did she say where she was going?"

"Nope. She just bought a ticket that got her on the bus."

"You don't know for where?" he said.

She looked at him from the tops of her eyes, but said nothing.

"Susan, tell me where Holly was going."

"I don't know where she was going, John. Judging by the way she acted, I don't think Holly knew either. Maybe she didn't want anybody to know, but she looked like she was in a hurry to get there."

"When was that?"

"The two-thirty-two."

It was now six-thirty. Four hours ago!

"All I can tell you is," Susan said, "the bus was headed east. Holly didn't say where she'd get off."

John bolted out the door, leaped into his truck and floor-boarded it. The only thing he knew for sure—he was headed east.

He didn't know where he'd wind up nor how far he'd have to go to get there, but Holly was out there some place, and he was going after her.

He didn't have to guess why she left. His grandmother's words echoed off the walls of his whirling brain. "Your mama ran your daddy off this place."

And his mother ran his wife off the place—four hours ago! John pushed the truck to move faster on the two-lane road, darting in and out of traffic, irate drivers' horns blaring in his ears.

Who did she know where she was going? She had no brothers nor sisters, and her parents died in that car wreck six years ago.

That left him nothing to go on.

He stopped at every place along the way where the bus might have dropped off a passenger, or picked up somebody beside the road, as buses often did in that part of the country.

He described Holly to everyone he saw: Five feet-three, chestnut hair, hazel eyes, hundred and fifteen pounds.

Had anyone seen a woman who looked like her? Thirty-four. Slender build. Gold-flecked grey eyes. Lips that drove him into fits of passion!

Most people boarding or getting off along the

way kept to themselves, minding their own business. Nobody remembered seeing the woman John described. How far he drove he didn't know.

At sunrise he spotted a Phillips gas station and turned in. He shoved the nozzle into the tank and pulled the trigger, hardly noticing when the gas overflowed onto the ground. He went inside to pay. He handed the white-haired man with no chin behind the counter a twenty-dollar bill.

John rubbed his weary eyes. "What time is it?"

The man looked past John's right shoulder at the clock on the wall behind him.

"Six-twenty-eight," the man said, counting out his change. "In the morning."

"Sixteen hours," John agonized.

"You all right, podnah?" the man said. "You look like you lost your last friend."

"My wife."

"You lost your wife?"

"She left without telling me where she was going. I've been looking for her all night."

"Well, I don't mean to be nosing in," said the man with no chin, "but you might want to leave it be. If she wanted to be found, you prob'ly wouldn't have to be looking for her."

John was in no mood for the man's homespun philosophy. He nodded, picked up his change, and headed for the truck.

A hundred times a day, he wished he'd been there when Holly left. They could have worked it out. Things happened to married couples all the time, and they worked them out. But he and Holly had no serious differences.

To hell with the farm! To hell with Clara! If Holly wanted to go, he'd have gone with her, if he'd known she was leaving.

None of that mattered now except that Holly was gone, and he didn't know where.

Etched on his memory were her provocative smile, and her soft hazel eyes with the gold flecks that told him how much she loved him. The husky voice, reassuring him with a comforting word when he needed it.

Across the meadow they'd raced, filling the warm night air with laughter. Skinny dipping in the catfish pond by the light of a midnight moon. The sheer ecstasy of waking at any hour of the night for love that couldn't wait. All this and more—so much more—she took with her.

Where was she now? What was she doing? With whom? A flood of questions, trailing wherever he went, kept him awake at night, but the answers never came.

What would Holly think if she knew he was spending time with Josie? He didn't dwell on it. Holly was set apart in a secret place, where nothing and no one could enter. Whatever he shared with Josie took nothing from what he reserved for Holly.

As he walked, he gave his head a bewildered shake. Clara and Holly. The two people in the world who meant most to him harbored no love for each other. It didn't take much for one woman to turn green over another.

With Holly out of her life, Clara's nemesis assumed a different name. Clara didn't know Josie, and knew nothing about her, except what the Parker sisters told her.

Oh, yes, John knew about the sisters. He was amused by what they thought was their secret spying. He'd seen them peeking out from behind drawn window curtains when he walked past their house on his way to Josie's. He suspected the little games the Parker spinsters played, reporting his arrivals and departures to Clara, were the only excitement in their sheltered existence.

The thought brought a wry smile to John's lips.

Chickweed and Johnson grass lined the ditches along the roadside.

Horned toads and lizards skittered in the dust, avoiding the little swirls of wind dancing between the corn rows. A cottontail dashed across the road in front of him as John lifted his head, squared his shoulders, and lengthened the strides taking him toward town.

Traffic was light most times, but Sunday night was for church goers in Blessing, especially for the Baptists. John had heard dozens of people "answered the call" as if Billy Graham had come to town. Many came to the altar at a recent revival meeting, and filled the pews for Sunday night preaching.

John stepped aside onto the gravel shoulder to avoid the whizzing traffic. A couple of cars slowed down and beckoned to him. He waved them on. A lift to town wasn't what he needed right then. Half way to Blessing, a gray Chevy pickup slowed down, pulled onto the shoulder, and waited for John to catch up.

John knew who was behind the wheel. Dude

Martin. Dude farmed the two-sixty south of John. With a wry grin, John shook his head. Why was Dude still driving that old Chevy truck with the front fenders rusted out? Dude separated from a couple of cantankerous wives, but he couldn't bring himself to part with that old truck. John caught up, and Martin thumbed him into the passenger side.

"You on your way to church, John?" Dude asked with half a grin. Dude was pretty sure John wasn't on his way to church, since he'd never known his neighbor to darken a church's door. John and Holly were married in the church, of course, and he went there for his grandparents' funerals, but those times didn't really count as "going to church."

"No," John said, climbing in. "I'm not going to church. But it looks like everybody else in the county is."

"Where are you headed?" Dude said.

John pulled his door shut. "To hell if I don't change my ways."

Dude cackled and swabbed his face with a red bandanna. "Ain't it dry though?" he said.

John didn't answer. Dude's obvious comment wasn't worthy of a response.

Martin shifted gears and moved the gray Chevy with the rusted fenders back onto the blacktop.

Dude bought his farm from Hamp Hargrove eleven years ago. Hamp quit farming after he got his left arm twisted off by a grain auger. The doctors tried to save it but gave up after a couple of months, sawed it off below the elbow, sewed it up, and sent Hamp home.

Some said Hamp spent the long recovery time

conditioning his imposing hulk to be even more intimidating and repulsive than what came naturally to the one-armed giant. Everybody, except John Willingham, believed that Seth Gibbs buried Hargrove in the Baptist church cemetery two years ago. Lately the word circulated that Hamp was miraculously resurrected and was back in Blessing, working for the Arkansas hog people at a job that didn't require two arms.

The Arkansas outfit was buying up thousands of acres of farm land for a massive hog breeding operation. Hamp's job was waving so much money under the farmers' noses it was impossible for them to resist.

John could testify to that, but didn't know whether Martin knew.

"Why, John," Dude said, keeping an eye on the road. "You seen Skelly Wilks lately?"

"This morning. He hauls my milk."

"Uh-huh. Mine too."

John could tell Dude was in a stew about something but didn't want to press too hard too fast.

Silence filled the cab. John knew Dude's patience was wearing to a frazzle, and wondered when he would get around to talking about it.

Skelly knew Hargove went out to the Willingham place, and it was a cinch the mayor told Martin about it when Skelly picked up Dude's milk that morning.

John waited, enjoying Dude's discomfort.

Dude was trying to work up some way to get at it without appearing to nose in, a tough chore since he was born nosy. Like the mayor, you didn't tell

Dude anything you didn't want anyone else to know.

Finally, Dude's curiosity pushed so hard he could no longer resist scratching the itch. "Why, John," he said, "did Skelly say anything to you about Hamp Hargrove? About Hamp being alive, I mean."

"He told me."

"Skelly told you, did he?"

"He didn't have to tell me."

"How's that?"

John wondered how much Martin knew. Dude was a good neighbor, but he wasn't easy to figure out. At times he thought Dude knew what he was talking about, and other times Dude acted like he didn't know anything. That was the face Dude was wearing now: The "I don't know nothin' about nothin" face. What he said was not always reliable, likely run through the shredder a few times before it got to him. "Hamp paid me a visit.

CHAPTER 4

"Hamp did? When was that, John?"

"A day or two ago."

John was on his way home from town when a big black GMC pickup crowded his rear bumper closer than was safe. The GMC followed him into John's lane, and braked to a stop behind where John parked his Ford next to the smokehouse.

John didn't know and didn't care what happened to Hargrove after Seth Gibbs buried that box two years ago, but he knew Hamp wasn't in it. To begin with, the box wasn't big enough to hold Hargrove's bulk.

Still, when John hopped out of his truck on his way to challenge whoever pulled up behind him, he was startled to see the grinning, one-armed giant stepping out of the GMC.

Hargrove was fifty-one years old. He stood six-feet-six and weighed over three hundred puffy pounds. He greeted John with a casual nod, and said it had been a long time. John agreed it had been. To himself he said it hadn't been long enough.

When they were neighbors years ago, John didn't have much use for Hargrove. Hamp borrowed his tools or equipment and didn't return them, and kept them so long he claimed they belonged to him. "What the hell are you doing?" John said.

"Howdy, John," said Hargrove with a sneaky grin.

"Were you trying to run over me?"

"Not exactly," Hargrove snorted. "I need to talk to you about selling the farm to some friends of mine."

"What do they want it for?" John said.

Hargrove sniggered like he thought John ought to know the answer already. His voice hardly above a hoarse whisper, he said, "To breed hogs on. You might want to give it a thinking."

Hargrove had more to say, hinting with a cobra smile that some people's houses might get burned down if they "didn't cooperate."

"They've got money, you got land," Hamp said. "Ought to be an easy move for a man that likes money more'n farming."

John let Hargrove know he wasn't interested, but said he would think about it.

Hargrove nodded, climbed in his truck, and left.

"You seen him?" Martin said, gulping, almost afraid to ask if John really saw a man who was supposed to be dead walking around.

John nodded.

"Well, I'll be damned!" Dude said. "Skelly mentioned it to me too, but you know Skelly. He sometimes don't recognize the truth even when he's telling it."

"Long on fancy and short on fact, Skelly is," John agreed.

Dude was itching to know what John and Hargrove said to each other, but balked at asking.

John let him stew.

Martin was several years older than John. His tousled brown hair stuck out from under a straw hat frayed around the edges. Dude's faded cotton shirt and blue-and-white striped Big Smiths struggled to keep from splitting in the middle of his watermelon waist. Tobacco-stained teeth protruded when he talked, and his heavy eyebrows hooded deep-set green eyes.

Dude was allergic to silence where two or more were gathered together, and after a minute or so of not hearing anybody talking, he was overcome with gall.

"What did old Hamp come to see you about, John?" he asked.

John enjoyed a private grin. Dude finally worked up the gumption to ask a direct question about what he wanted to know. "He was trying to get me to sell out to some hog outfit."

"Yeah?"

"I told him I wasn't interested. It's not my place anyhow. It's Mama's."

"Was it kinda skeery, John?

"How's that?"

"Well, you know. Old Hamp being dead and

all."

"He wasn't dead when I saw him."

"But he was buried, you know."

"I know Hamp was gone for a while after that shooting deal," John said, "but I never believed what Seth buried was him. When he was out at my place, he was still as big and ugly and overbearing as ever."

"Still didn't have no left arm?"

John cast him a tolerant look. "Hamp hasn't had a left arm for twelve years. You ought to know that better than anybody, since you bought his place. But he could still knock you all the way to Oke City and back with the other one."

"What are you aiming on doing?"

"About what?"

"Skelly said something about Hamp making a threat to you."

"You mean about burning my house down?"

"I believe it was something like that."

"That's Skelly all right. If you've got something you want the world to know, tell Skelly it's a secret. How the hell he ever got to be mayor I'll never figure out. Biggest blabbermouth in the county. He'll likely come back from the grave to tell something he forgot."

Dude gave that a cackle. He squirmed around, wearing a hole in the seat of his Big Smiths, trying to think of something important to say.

In the distance, lights popped on in Blessing like stars testing their brightness in the gathering dusk of a Sunday evening. Town was not far away. "Town" was Blessing. Most of the 957 souls who called it home were born there, and most of them wouldn't live any place else if they got paid for it. Of course, some of the younger ones went away when they got old enough to think they could take care of themselves without their parents eyeballing their moves. Others went seeking better opportunities in larger towns. Tulsa and Oklahoma City topped the list of places where jobs were more plentiful.

Some worked for thirty or forty years at Sears or the Post Office, better paying jobs than what they could find in Blessing, but moved back "home" when it came time to retire.

Dude's mind was not on Blessing. Sweat popped out on his wrinkled brow. He fidgeted, mopped his brow, and finally decided he'd better say what he wanted John to know before he let him off in town.

"Whereabouts can I drop you off at, John?"

"The Welcome Back is just down the road here a way. You might let me out there, if you don't mind."

"Oh, no, I don't mind at all. You gonna go see Josie?"

John's response was a sharp look. Dude's nose was too long. It was none of his business who John was going to see, though Dude probably knew anyway. Half the county knew John and Josie were keeping company.

Dude braked the Chevy to a stop in front of the Welcome Back Bar & Grill. "Why, John," Dude said, blurting it out like he couldn't wait any longer to get it said. "Hamp come to see me too."

John regarded him with a silent stare.

"He told me about that outfit in Arkansas," Dude said. "He said they had a wash tub full of money they wanted to spend on ground for some kind of hog operation around here. About what he told you, I'd judge."

John didn't mind Martin's nosing around till he found out what passed between himself and Hargrove. What he did mind was Dude's letting on like he knew nothing about the hog deal, nor that Hargrove wasn't dead. He tried not to explode in Dude's face, but it wasn't easy. "Well, Dude, have you thought about it?"

"Yeah, I give it a good thinkin'. Some of the other fellers—"

"What other fellas? You mean Hamp talked to— Who? Feely, McAnn, Burrell? What others are you talking about?"

"I believe he did say something about he talked to them."

"So, what did you and your friends decide?"

"To tell the truth, we was kind of waiting on you, John, since the water runs through your place."

"Is that what they want—the water?"

"Well, that and the ground with it, o'course."

"But, you haven't made up your mind yet what to do about it?"

"I wanted to talk to you first," Dude said. "We don't want to put nobody 'tween a rock and a hard place."

"Uh-huh," John grunted.

Dude gave his head a sorrowful shake. "No rain when we need it. Hog market down. It don't make no sense trying to outlive farming another year."

John wasn't surprised. Dude was the enemy of hard work. If he could sell his way out of the labor it took to make the farm pay, Dude would be the first in line. He received more government subsidies than anybody else in the county for not planting crops on the government's don't plant list.

John didn't blame Dude for that. The money was there for the taking. John accepted no subsidies because he didn't want some Washington bureaucrat who didn't know beans about corn telling him what to plant on his own ground.

"How come you played me along here, Dude?" John said. He was irritated, and Martin knew it. "Carrying on like you didn't know anything about that hog deal, and Hargrove being alive. How come you didn't just come right out and say Hargrove was trying to get you to sell out?"

Martin hung his head. "I don't know, John, I just—"

"Well, what are you aiming to do, Dude, you and your friends?"

"We're waiting for you, John. If you don't go, we don't go."

"Is that the deal—all or nothing?"

"If you don't go, the deal's off."

"Is that what Hargrove said?"

"That's what he said."

"And you're supposed to make me believe it's all right?"

Hargrove didn't tell John the Willingham place was the key to the package. So, if John couldn't talk his mother into selling the farm, the others stood to lose money from the sale of theirs. Even so, he never liked Hargrove, he didn't like the way Martin went about asking him what he already knew, and didn't like being the last to know the deal was dead if he didn't go along.

Not that it made any difference, John conceded to himself. Clara wouldn't go for it.

"You tell them I'll think about it," John said. He slid out of the truck, pinning Martin with a stern parting glare. "And, Dude—"

"Yeah?"

"Next time you've got something to say to me, you damn well better just say it straight out, instead of beating around the barn like a skulky fox."

"Oh, I will, John, you bet."

John watched him drive off. Maybe he owed it to the other farmers to at least think about it, and lay it out to Clara. He didn't have to guess what she'd say. When it came time for her to die, Clara would rather do it hunkered over the kitchen sink than spend the rest of her life rocking on the front porch of the old folks home in town.

John pushed open the door to the Welcome Back, and elbowed his way through the crowd to the bar. Loud music and raucous laughter weren't what he needed right then, but that's what he got.

The jukebox spouted Elvis's "Jail House Rock," drowning out conversation. All John wanted was to pick up a couple of burgers to take to Josie's for supper, and put the commotion of the Welcome Back behind him. He couldn't remember when buxom Lena Bradley hadn't tended bar and built burgers at the Welcome Back Bar and Grill. Lena greeted him with a broad, sweat-faced smile.

"What are you up to, John?"

"Oh, about six-two," he quipped

Lena laughed. "What can I do for you?"

"I need a couple of burgers about half cooked with everything."

"Onion?"

"You bet."

"A burger's not a burger without onion."

Lena was a fifty-year-old graying redhead whose breasts sagged to her forty-inch waist. In another hour she'd be off work. She'd go home to her daughter's three-month-old son Devon. Devon's unwed mother ran off with some hopped up, long haired loser who enjoyed the pleasure of fathering the child, but wanted nothing to do with him after the baby was born. Lena took on the responsibility of paying for baby sitters, diapers, and Pablum.

That was okay with Lena. What was not okay was that Betsy ran away to God only knew where and abandoned her baby son. She traded Devon for some deadbeat who'd dump her by the side of road when the thrill wore off.

Lena plopped John's burger patties on the grill and flipped them over a couple of times to be sure they were done on both sides. She spread the toasted buns with French's yellow mustard, and slapped burger patties on the toasted buns, sprinkled them with salt and pepper, and topped them off with pickle slices, lettuce, onion and tomato. She dropped the burgers and a handful of paper napkins into a brown bag, and handed it to John. "There you go. You gonna go see Josie?"

"Yeah."

"Tell her I said hi."

"I will. How's that boy doing?"

A smile lit Lena's sweat damp face. "Ah, he's doing great," she said. "Fat and sassy like his grandma."

John took up the bag and dropped some money on the counter, a little extra for the boy. On his way out he spotted Ernie Phipps at a table in the corner, pouring beer from a glass pitcher. John stepped over that way, and sat down at Ernie's table. He liked Ernie, and chatted with him occasionally when they bumped into each other.

Ernie greeted him with a smile-lit "Howdy."

"I hear you gave up rodeoing," John said,

"Yeah, I can't do that no more. I busted my leg up pretty bad. Me and old Son of Lightnin' got tangled up in Cheyenne, and he won. I'm over at the packing plant now."

"I heard about that," John said. "Why, Ernie, there's talk about an Arkansas outfit buying up land around here for some kind of hog operation. I thought you might have heard something about it at the plant."

Ernie nodded. "There's been talk. The last I heard Dude Martin was gung-ho for it."

"You talked to Dude, did you?"

"He made some mention of it one day last week when he brought a beef in. I got the idea he and some others are waiting to see what you're gonna do about it."

John knew that. He shook his head at how Dude strung him along. "What do you think about it?"

"Well, they tell me people where they've built them hog factories in other parts of the country don't like 'em. Too much stink and pollution."

"What kind of money are they talking about paying for ground?"

"It's hard to say. Prob'ly depends on how much dickering they can do with the farmers. But I hear they've got a barrel of money to spend on it." Ernie took a swallow from his beer glass. "Did you hear about Hamp Hargrove being alive?"

"Yeah," John said.

"Unbelievable. Hamp's working for that hog outfit now."

John figured Ernie told him everything he knew, and stood up to go. "If you decide to go back to bull busting," John said with a grin, "I've got one you can practice on."

Ernie laughed and waved him off. "Not with this bum leg," he said. "I ain't goin' down that road no more."

John said goodbye, worked his way to the door, and started walking toward Josie's. He wondered if she'd be home when he got there.

She was.

CHAPTER 5

Rufus tells Si Hamp ain't dead

Si Colby didn't know why Rufus Bonebrake was standing there staring at him with an anxious look on his face, fidgeting like a robin hen protecting her babies from a cat.

Si poured himself another cup of coffee from the black bottom pot, shuffled back to the big leather-bound recliner with holes worn in the arms and plopped into it.

He was in no hurry to find out what was burning Rufus's tongue. Most often when Rufus showed up, he was dragging a passle of bad news he couldn't wait to spill on somebody.

Etched on Si's memory was the time Rufus was in a sweat to tell him Si's thirty-seven-year-old son Isaac was accidentally shot and killed on that antelope hunt in Wyoming. Isaac was his and

Thelma's only son, the youngest of three children. That was the day Thelma began to die. A year later she did. Time would run out before Si got over it. He loved Isaac, but he worshiped Thelma. He doubted there was a grave deep enough to hold the load of sadness he'd take with him when they threw dirt in his face.

Rufus was fifty-nine years old, and skinny as a hungry snake. His brooding eyes reminded Si of a couple of holes burned into a stubble of beard. He was a Holy-Roller preacher until the day Elmo Holcomb caught him rolling around in the church basement with Elmo's wife Callie, the choir director. Elmo grabbed his weeping wife and hauled her home. He came back clutching a shotgun with the muzzle aimed at Rufus's Adam's apple.

Rufus's eyes got big as coffee cups. He was shaken to the toes of his twenty-nine-dollar Sears-Roebuck cowboy boots. Elmo pulled the hammer back on the gun and blessed Rufus with an assortment of uncomplimentary epithets.

Elmo squeezed the trigger and the twelve gauge misfired. Three times. Rufus interpreted that as some kind of miracle he was still breathing. He explained to Elmo, with what could be his last breath, he was spared by the Grace of God when the gun didn't fire.

Elmo figured if God had anything to do with it, he'd better spare Rufus too. Elmo packed up his twelve gauge and lit out for home. He apologized to the wayward preacher as he went, pleading forgiveness from the Almighty for coming damn near committing murder on a man of the cloth.

Even so, in the pulpit the following Sunday morning, the errant preacher coughed a time or two, cited failing health, and resigned as minister of the church. Since then, the only preaching Rufus did was to his hogs and cows in his muddy barn lot.

Simon sipped at his coffee, smacked his purple lips, and wiped the drippings from his chin. "Hot damn that's good!" he said. "My daddy used to say they wasn't but three real blessings in this world."

He paused to give Rufus time to ask what they were, but Rufus stared at him like he had no idea what Si was talking about. "A good old country crap when you have to," Simon went on, "a hot loving woman when you need to, and a steaming cup of coffee when nothing else will do you."

Rufus was not impressed with the philosophy of Si's dead father. He kept staring at Si, wondering how long it'd take him to get around to asking what he came for.

Simon had other things on his mind. "You was in the war, Rufus?" he said, postponing Rufus's bad news.

"Which one?"

"The big one. WW Two."

"Yes, sir, I was."

"Uh-huh," Si said. "I was always too young for the first one, and too old for the second one." Si's small dark eyes got smaller with a confidential squint as he leaned his balding gray head toward Rufus.

Rufus fidgeted some more. He knew when Simon looked like that he had a story to tell, and it would be a while before the storekeeper was ready to listen to what he came to say.

"Ever kill a man?" Si asked with an impish grin.

"I dunno. Can't say for sure," Rufus answered. He wondered why Si wanted to know something with nothing to do with why he waited for him to quit talking so he could.

"In the artillery where I was," Rufus said," we never seen many live ones. We just shot at what they told us to on the radio."

"The hell!"

In his bony hands, Rufus rolled his red corduroy cap with the flaps tied on top. "How about you, Si?" he said. "Ever kill a man?"

"Well now, they was this one jaybird. After my daddy died of heart failure, this feller named Henley Gore come around a-sparking my mama. I give him a wide berth for a time, 'cause him and me didn't see eye-to-eye on some things—like him squiring my mama.

"I still don't know why she was fool enough to let him hang around. Anyhow, I noticed they was getting pretty thick. One day my mama said to me, 'Simon, what'd you think if Henley and me was to get married?

"Well, I never figured she'd get wrapped up in no blanket with the likes of Henley Gore. Everybody knew he was worthless as tits on a boar. As it turned out, though, Mama was just telling me what was about to take place, and what I thought didn't amount to a hog fart in a whirlwind.

"Not long after that they got the knot tied at the Baptist Church. After the wedding, all Henley done was set around reading them western magazines, drinking beer, and smoking them filthy cigarettes.

"He put in a good'eal of time tormenting me and Mama too. One day I got a craw full of it, and I told Henley I didn't want to hear no more talk against my mama, or I was gonna rewind his clock and set it back a few notches. I could've done it too. I was a pretty big kid by then, but that didn't set well with old Henley. He took off into the house and come a-hollering back, waving my daddy's old squirrel gun like he was gonna use it on me. I grabbed up a stick of firewood and swang it at him, and caught him upside the head.

"Old Henley, he flopped around on the ground for a spell like a chicken with its head cut off, then he never moved no more.

"Mama seen the whole thing and screamed about it, and jumped up and down. When the time come, though, she told the judge ol' Henley, he come at me with the squirrel gun, and what I done was self-defense. The judge let me off. I think Mama was glad to get shut of that old devil. He wasn't good for nothing anyhow."

Rufus tried not to notice that Si fingered something from the corner of his eye.

"Well." Si sniffled and struggled to his feet. "I believe I'll have myself another cup of coffee."

"You want me to get it for you?" Rufus askws.

"Oh, hell no. If I ever get to where I can't pour my ownself a cup of coffee you can call the meat wagon and have me hauled away."

Si waddled over to the stove and poured his cup full. He didn't ask Rufus if he wanted a cup. He remembered how hot coffee made Rufus break out in hives. The last time he had a cup of Si's coffee Rufus's face got red and swollen, and Simon thought he was turning into some kind of monster. He called Doc Sloan, and Doc rushed right over.

With a tolerant sigh, the doctor prescribed, "No more coffee." Never since did Si offer Rufus any coffee.

Simon said, "Was there something you had on your mind, Rufus?"

"Yes, sir," Rufus said, relieved it finally was his turn to talk. "I come to find out if you know a man name of Hamp Hargrove."

Simon got a funny look on his face. He hadn't heard Hargrove's name mentioned for over two years.

"Used to know him," he said, "'fore he got dead."

"Well–uh–Hamp ain't dead, Si."

"The hell he ain't. I went to his burying my ownself."

"He ain't dead, Si."

"Come on, Rufus." A nervous chuckle escaped Simon's coffee wet lips. "You been hitting that drinking whiskey again, making you see things that ain't there?"

"What I hear," Rufus said, eyes wide with wonder. His voice rose with the excitement of his revelation. "Hamp was out to the Willinghams' trying to talk John into selling out to them hog people."

Simon seethed. He figured Skelly got to Rufus too. What was the world coming to, with folks spreading outlandish tales about a dead man not being dead? Simon was at the burying. He saw the box. Seth Gibbs said Hamp was in it. He saw Seth lower the box in the ground and throw dirt in on top of it.

Si gave his head a disgusted waggle. "Rufus, you know as well as I do Seth Gibbs buried that box with Hamp in it two year ago." He was so exasperated he needed a moment to catch his breath. "You shittin' me, boy? You're standing there telling me that seen him go to his everlasting grave I never seen Hamp Hargrove go to his everlasting grave?"

"Skelly Wilks said Hamp was out there trying to make a deal, but John didn't go for it," Rufus persisted. "Skelly said Hamp said he might burn John's house down if he didn't go along with the deal."

"Uh-huh," Si grunted, recalling his encounter with the dubious mayor. Coming from Skelly, it may or may not be true. "Skelly told you that, did he?"

"Skelly told me."

"How'd he find out?"

"He claimed John told him."

Si knew that. Skelly told him. Why John would tell Skelly anything besides how much milk he wanted him to haul was a stump Simon had trouble digging. John couldn't be that hard up for somebody to talk to.

Still, if John said it, there might be something to it. Simon never knew John to be anything but straight about whatever he said. Just like his daddy.

Kyle was a good man. He bought stuff from Simon on credit for years and never once failed to pay every penny he owed after he sold a crop.

Si recalled the day Kyle stopped by his place and told him he was leaving.

"I'm not going back out there," Kyle said. "And, Si—"

"Yeah, Kyle?"

"No need for anybody else to know."

Simon knew Kyle and Clara had problems. Most married couples did, but he figured they'd pass. He and Thelma disagreed at times too. Once in a while it looked like it might come to blows; though laying an angry hand on Thelma was the last thing Simon thought of doing. By morning they forgot whatever it was they disagreed about.

"Where you going?" Si had asked.

"I don't know. All I know is I'm gone. I'm telling you because somebody might ought to know in case it comes up sometime. You're the only one I can trust. I can't take any more of the stuff Clara keeps throwing at me."

Simon's eyes got wet, studying the harried face of his friend who determined at last to cast off the load he could no longer carry. "What about that boy?" Si asked. "You know John loves you more than anybody, Kyle. What's to become of him?"

Kyle hung his head and gave it a sad shake. He wiped his eyes and said nothing.

"What you're doing," Si said, "is it better than what you're running away from?"

"I'm not a strong man, Si." Kyle turned away. "I'm not a strong man."

Simon watched him slump back to his truck. Maybe Kyle was stronger than he knew.

From time to time over the years since Kyle left, Simon felt John's eyes on him from the other side of the meat counter. As if he was trying to see into Si's mind. Like he thought Si knew something nobody else knew. Maybe his father shifted his burden of humiliation onto the back of the storekeeper. Simon thought John was afraid to ask what he knew.

Sometimes Si was tempted to say to John, "Your daddy loved you, boy." He wanted to tell John what Kyle told him, but he dared not. Kyle trusted him not to tell anyone. Simon pulled himself away from the memory.

To Rufus, he said, "Have you talked to John about Hargrove?"

"No, sir. I talked to Skelly."

"Did Skelly want me to do something?"

"He figured you might want to have a talk with Hamp, and see if he really meant to burn John's house down."

"That's Skelly all right. There ain't nothing the mayor enjoys more than getting somebody else to do what he's supposed to do. "Hamp never was one to do much talking. Once he made up his mind to get something done, he usually got it done.

"Wonder why Skelly never went to the sheriff about this?"

"I dono," Rufus said. "Maybe he thought you could head it off, you know. Going to Limpy might make it look more serious than it is."

"Well, I figure if Hamp's got it in mind to burn

John's house down, that's pretty damn serious." Si took a swipe at the coffee drippings on his chin. "You know where Hamp lives?"

"I know where he used to live before he—you know."

"Why don't you go out there and see if Hamp's there? If he is, tell him my rheumatiz is backing up on me or I'd come out there my ownself. I need to settle this thing so I can get it off my mind."

Rufus shifted from one foot to the other. He didn't want to go. The thought of talking to somebody who was supposed to be dead made him queasy in the stomach.

"I ain't too good at that kind o' thing," he said.

Simon nodded as if he understood. "You seen Ernie Phipps lately?"

"I know he hangs out at the Welcome Back some."

"Go see if you can find Ernie. Tell him I need to talk to him. He don't have to know why."

"I'll do 'er, Si. If Ernie's there, I'll tell him."

Ernie feared neither man nor beast, dead or alive, Si mused as Rufus headed for the door.

Yeah. Ernie would take care of it.

CHAPTER 6

Clara pays Josie a visit

To Clara, the eleven-year-old Pontiac was a challenge. Even so, she was determined to get it moving so she could carry out her mission. She made up her mind it was her responsibility to rescue her son from the clutches of that evil woman, and there was no time to lose getting it done. The best way to do it was to get eyeball-to-eyeball with evil. She would fly to the yellow bungalow on the wings of the aged Pontiac.

That was, if she could get it started and moving in the right direction, of which she was not at all sure, since she never drove it before. Two lessons with John's prodding didn't teach her everything she needed to know about driving the Pontiac. She was too strong-willed (John called it stubborn) to sit still long enough for him to teach her what to do.

Clara insisted he leave her alone to do it

herself. Though her confidence was weak as a spider web, she had to try. This was one of those emergencies for which John told her when she might need to know how to drive.

Before Kyle left, she didn't need to know, because he took her wherever she wanted to go. But, Kyle skipped out, and her father and mother came to live with her while John was off fighting those heathens in Korea, and grandpa did the driving. Her father admonished Clara that it wasn't safe for her to drive on the public road. He never said whose safety he tried to protect.

Clara didn't trust Holly behind the wheel. The one time she rode with Holly, out of sheer fright, Clara sat stiff-legged, both feet jamming the floorboard, her heart pounding as if it might split her girdle. She was dead certain disaster was looming around the next curve, for which Holly wasn't inclined to slow down. After that first hair-raising experience, Clara promised herself she'd never ride with her daughter-in-law again, and she didn't.

John drove her now when she needed to go some place, mostly to drop her off at church on Sunday morning, or to Si Colby's Sak 'n Pak every week or so, relieving her of the need to learn to drive.

But, this time John was gone, and she was glad. He would have tried to stop her from doing what the Lord told her must be done.

She hoped she wouldn't run into John on the way to town. The first thing she had to do was get the Pontiac backed out of the shed, onto the road, and aimed toward Blessing. She wasn't sure she could do it, but she was determined to give everything she had to the effort.

Making it safely into town and back, she thought, would be no big deal. That she had no driver's license was a minor consideration, had she even thought of it. She'd be to town and back before anybody knew she was gone.

It was only a few minutes' drive each way. What she had to say to that woman would take less time than pressing a napkin. She'd say what she came to say, emphasize strongly the need for Josie to stay away from her son, and be out of there on her way home, and nobody would ever know.

The only thing that could stop her was the commanding voice of God Almighty Himself. She discussed her plan with Him when she woke up at three o'clock in the morning. He didn't tell her not to go, so she took it as a sign she'd better go full steam ahead, and get it done.

It took her a moment to find the ignition, but once she got the key stuck in the right place and the engine started, she remembered to press the clutch to shift gears. She wiggled it into reverse and stepped on the gas, pleased with herself for getting the car out of the shed without ramming into the maple tree. After a series of body-jarring bucks and jolts, she finally got the Pontiac pointed toward town. She felt more at ease behind the wheel.

What she was about to do weighed heavily upon her mind as she drove, careful to stay on her side of the yellow line, as John instructed. Her son was a kind and considerate man who avoided conflict, just like his daddy. Living with Kyle was easy because he never fought back. Clara perceived Kyle's peace-loving nature as weakness.

John wasn't weak, but he never did anything to hurt anybody, she mused. He kept going to see Josie, Clara rationalized, only because he didn't want to hurt her by breaking off their relationship—whatever that was. As a boy, John often brought home stray dogs and cats, and was always ready to lend a hand when a neighbor needed help.

That Josie woman was a stray, Clara counseled herself, and she strayed too far from the straight and narrow to be any good for her son. Josie was thirty-six-years old. The older some folks got, the blinder they got, and John suffered an acute case of blindness over that woman.

Clara was blinded by the determination to fight for her son while there was still time to save him. Josie Cramer was a blight on the face of the earth. Of course, Clara never met Josie, but she knew her kind.

During the Big War, when grandpa was still able to take care of the farm, Clara and her friend Patsy Bye volunteered to work two days a week cleaning up after the night before at the USO over at Tahlequah. Talk about man hunters! Clara worked with them. She almost threw up listening to their disgusting brags about their escapades of the night before. If they wanted a man, they knew where to find him, and jabbered about it all the next day.

Josie Cramer was as bad as those women. Maybe worse. The Parker sisters convinced Clara the world would be a better place to live without

Josie Cramer in it. Clara's intent was to eliminate her from the world of John Willingham.

Hunched over the steering wheel, Clara gripped it so tight her knuckles turned white, as if it might get away if she relaxed her hold on it.

She wasn't sure how she'd broach the matter once she stood face-to-face with "that woman," but she depended on the Lord to tell her what to say.

The last thing she wanted was to see her boy corrupted by some low-life woman of the world.

She didn't known how to talk to Holly either. Holly went two years to the university at Norman before she married John, and Clara was intimidated by her.

Oh, she was nice enough in the beginning, Holly was. But she spent too much time with John, riding around the field with him on that tractor, curling up on his lap, watching TV while Clara cleaned up after supper. Clara resented Holly. Before John and Holly married, Clara had him to herself. Afterwards, Holly occupied most of John's time, and all Clara could do was watch with envious eyes, and stew about it.

The first comfortable breath she had drawn in years was on the day Holly left. And, of course, John blamed his poor little old mother for that. He hadn't been there to talk Holly out of leaving when she decided to go, and Clara didn't try. She'd have helped her saucy daughter-in-law pack if it would have hurried her departure.

Clara grumbled that John was cut from the same cloth as Kyle. It never occurred to Kyle to defend himself against her in an argument. He just sort of smiled and turned back to whatever he was doing before. She loved Kyle, but she'd have respected him more if he'd shown more grit, reacting with anything short of body blows. But, Kyle took off the same way Holly did, without telling anybody where he was going, nor even that he was leaving.

Kyle was gone, Holly was gone, and Clara was happy to have her son to herself again. Except for Josie, and Clara heard enough about her to know it was time she took matters in her own hands, and faced up to the brazen hussy in the yellow bungalow.

Millie Baucum didn't get it done, and didn't have the guts to do it herself. Nor did Millie have a son caught like a 'possum with its foot in a trap.

Clara's message from the Lord urged her to take care of the Josie matter before it was too late. The Lord pointed a divine finger at her and told her she was doing the right thing. Clara was certain He was riding on the seat beside her. By the time she arrived at Josie's, the Lord would tell her what He wanted her to say.

On the corner of Fourth and Elmwood, Clara spotted Josie's yellow bungalow, right where the sisters told her it was. She slammed her foot on the brake, and the Pontiac skidded sideways, bounced off the curb, and died. Half her mission, just getting there, was accomplished.

Clara breathed a deep sigh. She took a moment to study the neat little house where red geraniums flourished in full bloom around the front porch, and the blue morning glory vines climbed up the side of the house. That was not the kind of place Clara expected to find Josie Cramer living in.

She didn't know what whores did to fill their time, but, in Clara's mind, it was not supposed to be spent tending flowers, digging weeds out of the beds, and painting the outside of the house a soft yellow color so pleasing to the eye. Lounging around half naked, smoking cigarettes and drinking beer maybe, but not this.

Clara's determination began to waver. She wondered briefly whether she picked the wrong house to march up to the front door and ring the bell. But this was where the sisters said she'd find the home of Josie Cramer. She had come this far, she rationalized, and was honor bound to carry through with her plan. She crawled out of the Pontiac and strode briskly along the cobblestone walkway to the front door.

On the way there she breathed a prayer that God would not desert her. Satisfied that He didn't, she pressed a thumb to the bell and waited. Her courage was bolstered by the assurance that it was the right thing to do.

The door swung open, and in it stood a young woman. She was younger than Clara expected. Maybe thirty-five. Small of stature, dark wavy, just-shampooed hair sweeping her shoulders, clear complexion, flashing a disarming smile.

"Yes?" the young woman said.

Clara was taken aback. She envisioned being greeted by some harsh, gaudy foghorn in flimsy black lace underwear befitting her vision of a woman of the world, which she perceived Josie to be.

"Are you Josie Cramer?"

"Yes, ma'am, I'm Josie."

"I'm John's mother."

"John's mother? Oh, Mrs. Willingham!" She drew her blue chenille robe closer under her chin.

"I'm not very presentable. I just got out of the tub."

Clara couldn't have cared less what she just got out of. She had a job to do, and nothing could stop her from getting it done.

"How nice of you to come," Josie said. "John isn't here. I haven't seen him for a while, but I thought he might be coming tonight."

Clara's confidence soared. It would be less messy without John.

"Is there something wrong?" Josie said. "Can I tell John you were here?"

"No." Clara flung the screen door open, pushed roughly past the smaller woman, and barged into the front room.

"You're the one I want to talk to," she said.

CHAPTER 7

A look back for Josie

Simon Colby quipped that in Springer, seven miles down the road east of Blessing, "There are more dogs than people."

Most of Springer's 170 residents were pensioners, retirees, and welfare recipients. They passed the time rocking on their front porches when the weather was good, and peered with glazed eyes through curtainless windows when it was not.

In good weather or bad, three hours a day they shared the pain of the radio characters "Oxydol's Own Ma Perkins" and "Young Doctor Malone," among radio soap operas depicting lives even more depressing than their own.

In Springer, the rumble of Santa Fe trains no longer shattered the midnight silence. The sound of children's laughter was as rare as an eclipse of the moon, and averting the aimlessness of tomorrow was as unlikely as snow in July.

In the "old folks home" residents longed for a postcard, a letter, a phone call, or a visit from a loved one—anything to brighten the dullness to which they could visualize no end.

Rarely did they look beyond tomorrow. Every morning they awoke with the hope for one more day. They yearned for assurance that they had not been forgotten, relegated to a world of gray wrinkles, and arthritis-twisted limbs. Nighttime slumber and daytime naps did little to help them escape a life of boredom in a dying town.

Except to "dry up and blow away," there was little promise they'd find relief from the sedentary life that began the day they were helped through the front door of "the home" by a relative no longer able to care for them—or who was relieved to rid himself of an elderly parent, a detriment to his family's life style. Residents long since became resigned to the hopelessness of having nothing to get up for each morning.

It was not always so. When Josie Cramer was growing up there, Springer bustled with activity. Five times as many people called it home, and the winning high school basketball team gave them something to shout about. Josie was Homecoming Queen her senior year. Her father, pastor of the Springer Baptist Church, met her in the middle of the basketball court and proudly escorted his daughter to the podium to receive her crown. Joy ran rampant in the city of Springer, exemplifying life in small town America.

Then one day the Santa Fe ripped up its rails,

hauled them away, and the trains stopped stopping. Not long after, the Farmers Association closed its feed mill, the grocery, hardware and clothing stores locked and barred their doors. Churches gave up the struggle to keep their doors open.

Springer, as did many small towns across the country, depended on the railroad to stay alive. Faced with the inevitable gasping for breath, it was now the ghost of a once thriving community.

Si Colby was heard to remark that Springer was nothing more than a rumor mill where "you could hear anything but bacon frying.'

Such was the desolation to which Josie Cramer returned. She viewed with sadness the deterioration of the thriving community she departed years before, and turned away from the town she once called home. But she could not walk away from the memories of her childhood in Springer.

Growing up, she was frightened by her mother's complaining of various ailments, any one of which, she was assured, could prove fatal before the week was out. In her waning hours (at least twice a week) Josie's mother brought her young daughter to tears by declaring with trembling lips, "You'll never see me again," because she was certain that she would be gone before sunrise.

She also warned Josie of the "evils of men. Don't ever trust a man." Josie wondered if her mother's warning against men included her father whom she idolized, and whether the dire admonition, adversely, painted an attractive picture drew Josie into a world where men sought her favors.

How she managed to outlive the fears instilled by her mother, and what path led her to the realm of prostitution, only Josie knew. Perhaps it was a bridge between her mother's condemnation of men and her learning the truth about them.

Fear of her parents' righteous indignation, had they known of her worldly ways, was greater than her fear of the wicked world her mother reviled.

At some point along the way, Josie grew weary of "working the camps," as the Parker sisters, unable to utter the word "whore" described their new neighbor's former endeavors. Josie perceived her retirement as the end of an era, during which she unabashedly "brought joy to lonely soldiers far from home."

It wasn't clear to which of her myriad afflictions Josie's mother finally succumbed. Not long after her death, failing health forced Josie's father to give up his ministry at the Springer Baptist Church. A few months later he died of what the doctor called "internal complications."

Learning of her father's death hastened Josie's return to Springer. She decided it was time she renewed her acquaintance with the simple surroundings of her childhood. However, distressed that in her absence the pulse of Springer slowed to near lifelessness, she chose to settle in nearby Blessing, where, she promised herself, nobody would care where she came from, nor what she did before to earn a living.

One night at the Welcome Back Bar & Grill she caught sight of a man she never saw before. She'd soon learn he was John Willingham, sitting alone at a table, contemplating the loss of his runaway wife. Newcomer Josie didn't know about Holly when she invited herself to a seat at his table.

"Mind if I join you?" she said.

John said of course not. He pulled out a chair, and she sat on it. During the course of their learning about each other, Josie told him she moved to Blessing after several years away and knew nobody in town.

With no parents left to be horrified by her questionable past, Josie made no attempt to conceal from John the fact that she plied her trade within earshot of military bases. Josie kept no secrets, sharing with John the intricacies of a shadowy past for which she evinced no remorse, as though by revealing her previous life, she opened the door to the future.

John commended her. While he was in the army, he was stationed near a couple of the camps she mentioned. She made it clear her former life was just that, and had no plans for resuming it in Blessing, Oklahoma.

John admired her honesty and candor, and so, as two unencumbered souls, they touched casually on the possibility of "meeting again sometime". They did, three nights later. Thus began a relationship that lasted for the better part of two years.

Josie's assumption about the people of Blessing was only half right. Nobody asked about her past, but somehow the word got around. News of a new woman in town spread like water on a flat rock.

The Parker sisters somehow learned Josie once

"worked the camps," and couldn't wait to broadcast the news of a "professional setting up shop" on the corner of Fourth and Elmwood in the city of Blessing. To a town full of God-fearing people, a lady "professional" meant only one thing: Her body was for sale.

The new woman in town soon became the prime topic of conversation—and often gossip—at the Pak 'n Sak store, Dixie's Do Drop Inn, even dominating the ladies' afternoon teas and sewing circles.

Among the men of the citizenry, Josie Cramer was a favorite topic, referred to with rare enthusiasm. Not so with their women. In the Ladies' Circle of the Methodist Church, mention of Josie's name was received with misgiving.

"A blight on the face of the earth!" proclaimed Millie Kern, Circle president.

Millie, tall and thin with a mole dominating her left cheek, and vengeance in her eyes, was certain that her husband Hiram would be vying for a place in line, awaiting his turn at Josie Cramer's bedroom door. Millie proposed forming a committee to "pay that woman a visit and find out what she's up to."

Gladys Blaylock, plump and timid, wondered, "What are we gonna do if we don't like what she says?"

"Well—well–" Millie stammered. "Let's find out what it is first."

For lack of support from women who didn't want "to get involved," and others who were embarrassed that Millie even broached the matter, the protest died an early death. No committee was formed, and the campaign never got off the ground when no one volunteered to confront "that hussy" in the yellow bungalow.

Millie's motion faded with the sunset.

Benny Pelham, the twenty-nine-year-old editor of the Blessing Blessing, stopped by the Sak 'n Pak to get a statement from Simon Colby, the city's elder statesmen. Benny wanted to publish Simon's opinion of the town's newest resident.

Benny's journalistic position was, as Blessing's venerable citizen, the town should be made aware of Simon's perception of the young woman who paid cash for the yellow bungalow that stood empty and unsold for two years before she came to town.

"It might give the economy a shot in the arm," Simon said with a twinkle in his eye. "There hasn't been this much excitement in Blessing since Tom Mix come by years ago."

"Tom Mix?" Benny never heard of the fabled cowboy actor.

"Old time movie star," Si said. "He come by here one day back in the Thirties, and stayed all night at the boarding house. He shook my hand same as you did. Common as home-made soap." Si paused for a swig of coffee. "You can tell the folks not to worry about that lady," he said. "If she's a hinder, we'll know it soon enough. If she's not, she needs to be left alone."

The people of Blessing soon discovered the merits of Simon's appraisal. Josie gave money to the local library, and contributed to a fund for the repair of the hardwood floor in the high school gym.

In memory of her late father, Josie offered a

donation to the Springer Baptist Church. However, the church's new minister, the Reverend Clovis Groop, refused to accept the donation on the grounds it was "tainted by its evil source." Even so, Groop became downright irate upon learning the Blessing Presbyterian Church suffered no such restraint, and welcomed Miss Cramer's contribution of five thousand dollars. The Presbyterians deduced that if Josie could so freely part with that amount of money, surely somewhere along the way both she and it were cleansed of all evil.

Because of her generosity, and because she hadn't paraded her perfumed wares down the middle of Main Street—as some wary souls predicted she might—the town finally convinced itself the once-upon-a-time woman of the world was no longer practicing her former profession in the city of Blessing. The community wasn't contaminated by her presence, and even the women came to respect Josie's unspoken intent not to lure the local males into a lover's trap.

Millie Kern remained an adamant exception to those wives who breathed more easily, convinced as she was that one day she'd have to call the local cop to drag her husband from the bosom of that vicious woman.

Except for Millie and Limpy Logan, the citizenry thanked Josie for contributions she made to the improvement of their city, and paid her but little more attention than long-standing citizens, respecting her as they respected each other.

When she moved into the yellow bungalow, the deputy sheriff called on Josie a time or two.

Speculation ran rampant as to whether Limpy's visits were official or social. Limpy protested that his calls to the Cramer residence were strictly business, giving rise to the obvious query: His or hers?

Limpy threatened to turn in his badge, but he couldn't find it.

CHAPTER 8

John finds Josie at home

The reflection brought a wry smile to the lips of John Willingham as his walk from the Welcome Back took him to Josie's front door, bearing the brown paper bag of Lena Bradley's hamburgers.

Up the steps he went, and gave the bell button a healthy shove.

There was no answer. He tried again. Still no answer.

It wasn't like Josie not to be home on a Sunday evening. He opened the screen door and tried the doorknob.

The door eased open. He stepped inside.

Greeted by silence, he called, "Josie."

Across the living room he strode, and into the hallway leading to Josie's bedroom.

"Josie."

He eased open her bedroom door and peeked

inside.

"Josie!"

On the floor beside her bed lay the crumpled nude body of Josie Cramer.

CHAPTER 9

David meets Goliath

"Are you Hamp Hargrove?"

Ernie Phipps had no idea what he might run into as he walked up the weed-infested gravel leading to the front door of the small frame house on the south edge of town. Growing up in Blessing, Ernie knew of Hampton Hargrove. But, rodeoing took him all over for several years, and he could remember no words passing between himself and the one-armed giant.

Si Colby was bedrock certain he saw Hargrove go to his "everlastin' grave." In case Si was right, Ernie was in no hurry to go looking for the flabby Hargrove to find out if he was dead or alive. Even so, if Si Colby asked him to do something, Ernie didn't hesitate to get it done. Ernie would always remember what Simon did for him in his early days of bull riding.

Back when Ernie decided to try his luck on the rodeo circuit, there were entry fees, meals, travel expenses, and motel bills to pay. More than once, Si slipped him money "till you get on your feet," sometimes as much as a hundred dollars. Ernie always paid him back any time he had a good day wrestling bulls, but he still owed Si a debt of gratitude for his help when he needed it most.

Si never told anybody what he did for Ernie, just as he didn't mention that he was the only person Kyle Willingham told he was leaving town.

If you had a secret you wanted to stay that way, you didn't tell Skelly Wilks—you told Simon Colby.

As a kid, Ernie was lean and scrawny, as if he never had enough to eat to make him big. He was so quiet and timid some kids in school got a kick from poking fun at him. One day Ernie came home scratched up and crying. His father whacked him across the backside with a leather belt for not fighting back.

"Even if you don't win," his father threatened with a scowl, "don't you come home crying to me, boy, if you don't fight back."

Ernie would never forget the lesson. Sometimes he came home battered and bruised. His father looked at him with a funny grin, like he couldn't believe his kid had the guts to fight back. But he never again saw Ernie cry. Even when his mother died when he was nine, Ernie didn't cry.

The little guy promised himself when he grew up he'd be so tough nothing, and nobody, could hurt him. When he got old enough, he got tough by riding wild rodeo bulls, what the professional riders called the toughest sport on dirt.

Ernie didn't win many purses, but he won enough to keep him in the game. He worked harder than anyone else because he had to. He strained every muscle in his slight body to stay aboard fifteen-hundred pounds of leaping, fish-tailing, wild-eyed bull doing everything it could to make sure Ernie didn't hang onto the flank strap for the eight-second eternity required to win.

Ernie didn't figure Hargrove, dead or alive, would be any tougher to get along with than a raging bull.

The big man with no left arm filled his doorway with his six-foot-six, three-hundred-eighty pound bulk. Hargrove's graying hair was tousled as if he just crawled out of bed.

With piercing eyes, Hamp squinted down at the little man looking up at him.

"Who the hell wants to know?" was Hamp's response to Ernie's inquiry. Hamp's wheezy voice sounded like he was about half way into a four-day drunk.

"I do," said Ernie.

"Who the hell am I talking to?"

Through the screen door, Ernie thought Hargrove looked like a mass of strained flab in brown corduroy pants. Hamp's long, broad, white-stockinged feet were shoeless. His face hadn't been shaved for a week, and his dingy white, long handled underwear was unbuttoned at the throat.

"Ernie Phipps," the little man said.

Phipps was five-feet-eight inches tall and

weighed in at a hundred-forty-four pounds. Being tossed into the air and mauled by the head and horns of rampaging monsters broke half the bones in his body. Those were the times when he was driven by the glaring image of his dead father, still screaming at him. Times when he was thrown by a bull before the eight seconds passed, Ernie couldn't wait to "get back up there and do'er again." Every time he straddled the back of that beast, and grabbed the flank strap with a gloved hand, he saw his father scowling at him, yelling, "Don't come crying to me, boy, if you don't fight back!"

Ernie's rodeo career ended at Cheyenne's Frontier Days when a bull named Son of Lightnin' crushed his right leg against the arena wall. He didn't realize his dream of becoming a world champion bull rider, but he never met a bull too big or too wild to challenge. Respected by his peers as a tough little competitor, what Ernie lacked in talent, he made up for in guts and perseverance.

"I don't know you," Hargrove roared. "What the hell are you doing here, pounding on my front door?"

Ernie said, "Si sent me to find out if you was dead or alive."

"Si—"

"Colby."

"Well, hell, boy, you're standing there looking at me. Am I dead or alive?"

Phipps blinked.

Hamp said, "You say Si sent you?"

"He did. You gonna let me in, or do I have to do it from here?"

"Do what?"

"Si says talk to you, and that's what I'm aiming on doing."

Ernie's audacity wrenched from the bowels of the Hargrove flab a derisive chuckle.

He held the door open and stood aside to let the little guy pass.

To Ernie, Hargrove's front room looked like it lost a couple of rounds with a buffalo stampede, cluttered beyond livability. Chairs were piled high with old newspapers and outdated Playboy magazines with yellowed pages. Empty beer cans littered the floor, and glass ashtrays overflowed with cigarette butts.

In the center of the room stood a huge sofa with ugly slashes in its leather upholstery. On the white plastered walls hung black-and-white photographs of Pretty Boy Floyd, John Dillinger, Baby Face Nelson, Bonnie and Clyde, and other gangsters of the notorious Twenties and Thirties. A black cat scampered through an open door, seeking safety from the odor of evil.

"So, old Si sent you out here, did he?" Hargrove said.

"He did."

"How come Si didn't come?"

"Si don't get around too good any more. Rheumatiz, he said. 'Course, Si's fat too."

Hargrove interpreted that as a condemnation of his own blubber, but he let it pass.

"What was it you come to see me about, boy?" he said, letting Ernie know it was time to get down to it.

Ernie bristled. He didn't like being called boy by anybody, big or little. But Si sent him on a mission, so he didn't push it.

"Si says he went to your burying," Ernie said.

"Yeah?"

"He says he seen you put in the ground."

"No."

"In that wooden box, Si says."

"Hell, boy, use your eyes. Who do you think you're looking at?"

"Si says he seen them throw dirt on that box with you in it, and everybody walked away crying and sniffling, carrying on something awful."

Hargrove's response was a menacing smirk.

"Are you saying you wasn't in that box?" Ernie persisted.

"What did you say your name was?"

"Phipps," Ernie said, standing his ground. "Ernie Phipps."

"Well, Ernie Little Shit Phipps, I don't know you. If I did know you, I wouldn't like you, and if I don't like you, I don't tell you a damn thing." He pressed a fat fist against Ernie's chin, stretching his neck with an upward motion.

Ernie squinted at him through half closed eyes.

"Any more questions?" Hargrove asked.

"You ain't gonna tell me you was in that box?" Ernie gasped.

Hargrove removed his fist, glaring at Ernie with a mean eye. "Who the hell do you think you are," Hamp roared, "nosing around in something that's none of your damn business?"

"Si sent me to find out."

"Ask me if I give a shit who sent you!"

"Si seen you in that box."

"No, Si never seen me in no box because it was never opened!"

"You wasn't in it?"

"Hell, no, I wasn't in it!"

Hargrove wiped his mouth and took a moment to cool off. This little gnat was getting to him, and he didn't like it. He couldn't believe he hadn't already broken him across his knee for his nagging impudence. If he had, he wouldn't have to put up with his persistent gouging. "You tell old Si I wasn't in that box. You tell him there was nobody in that box Seth Gibbs buried that day."

"Well, then—-"

"Aw, hell, it don't matter now? The whole town will know about it anyhow. You see, Bernie—-"

"Ernie."

"—some people wanted me dead real bad because of something that happened back in—-" He broke off his narrative. "Will you explain something to me, boy? Why the hell am I taking up my valuable time talking to you?"

"'Cause I was fixing to bash your damn head in if you never."

Hargrove glared, unblinking, into the dauntless face of the man less than half his size. He tried to convince himself that he hadn't heard what his ears were asking him to believe escaped the lips of this miniature human being with the gall of a riled rattler.

Hargrove smiled. He chuckled. He laughed out

loud at the thought of little Ernie Phipps bashing the head of the intimidating one-armed giant before whom men twice Ernie's size cringed. Hargrove laughed until he was weak. He roared so hard he stumbled onto the rickety sofa and it collapsed under his massive weight.

Ernie said, "What do you want me to tell Si?"

Hargrove finally regained control, stumbled to his feet, and looked down at Ernie with a jaundiced eye. "You know what I like about you?" Hargrove said. "Not a damn thing. You don't tell Si nothin'. When I get around to it, I'll go see him and tell him myself."

Satisfied that he'd done his job, Ernie turned on a heel and headed for the door.

"And, boy," Hargove said, "if I ever see you again, you better be crawling to me on your hands and knees, begging for mercy."

Into the squinting eyes of Goliath, little David stared with unmitigated gall.

"Up your ass, fat boy," Ernie said on his way out.

CHAPTER 10

Louise, Josie is dead

Limpy Logan wasn't really the sheriff, but people called him that, and he liked it. As a deputy, he was the nearest thing to law enforcement Blessing had going for it. Well, it would be a stretch to say Blessing had Limpy going for it, since sheriffing didn't eat up a lot of his time. Crime was the one thing Blessing had the least of, not counting the absence of a McDonald's and Walmart, and worried least about. Topping the list of Limpy's favorite things were bass fishing and coon hunting. When he wasn't bass fishing or coon hunting, chances were he pulled the covers over his head and dreamed about bass fishing and coon hunting.

Resting was one thing Limpy did best. At a hundred-thirty-seven pounds, his energy played out in a hurry. He was known to get plum tuckered just walking from his bathroom to the bedroom, often reminded right away that it was nap time

To "establish a presence" in Blessing, the county provided Logan with the luxury of Louise Whitworth's telephone. Limpy didn't have a phone and didn't want one. He once had a phone, but all it was good for was for some stranger to ring him up, wake him out of a deep sleep, and try to sell him something he didn't want.

Louise lived next door to Limpy. Any time somebody called for the sheriff, which was less often than a solar eclipse, Louise yelled at him out her west window to Limpy's east window. If Limpy wasn't fishing or hunting, or still asleep at any hour of day or night, he might respond.

The last time Louise had a call for the sheriff was the previous Spring when the widow Butler's cocker spaniel got a foot caught in a muskrat trap.

Limpy finally squeaked a sleep-laden "hullo" out his window at three o'clock in the afternoon. While Louise was explaining what she called him for, Limpy dozed off again.

"Sheriff, do you hear me?" she screamed so loudly she was afraid it might shatter neighborhood light bulbs.

With a disgusted effort, seeing his beady eyes squinting between the bottom of shade and the window sill, Louise convinced him he had an emergency call. Reluctantly, Limpy crawled out of bed, got dressed, and fed himself a cold baloney sandwich for lunch. When he arrived at the scene, he found the cocker dead of exhaustion trying to free itself.

That was the day Mrs. Butler found out what

stress was. Doc Sloan prescribed therapy.

It was sleeping the sheriff was doing Sunday evening when John Willingham called on Josie Cramer's phone to tell Limpy she was dead.

Louise asked John how long he could wait. John said there was no hurry. Nothing could be done for Josie anyway.

Louise yelled out her west window, hoping Limpy might be conscious. After the fourth yell, Limpy rolled over, knuckled the sleep out of his eyes, and stuck a tousled head up over the window sill, trying to focus on Louise's face.

Louise nodded, signifying that she recognized Limpy's head. She went back to the phone on the kitchen wall beside the refrigerator. Into it, she said to John, "He's comimg."

"When?"

When was a question for which Louise had long since given up seeking an answer. In the seven years she was employed by the county as Limpy's keeper, she longed for the days of her childhood when there were only snakes, tarantulas, and black widow spiders to put up with. Two divorces and five kids later, she never considered leaping to freedom from the Cimarron River bridge until after she retired as a nurse from the funny farm, and moved next door to Limpy Logan. Louise struggled still with the disbelief that he wasn't one of the inmates into whose mouth she shoveled corn meal mush at the farm.

For sixty-three years Louise eluded the curse of gray hair, jagged nerves, obesity, and occupational stress. Then one day the county came up with enough money to pay her for babysitting the hapless deputy. Many times since, she asked herself if she would do it again. The answer was etched on her brain: Only if they raised her Social Security enough to cover the cost of pills that kept her sane.

To John, she said into the phone, "I don't know when. All I know for sure is that he's still breathing. If you're lucky, and if he doesn't get a sudden urge to wet a hook, you might see him sometime in the next day or two."

"Louise—"

"You know Limpy, John. He doesn't do anything in a hurry. It's too taxing on the brain."

John was getting edgy. "Louise—"

"John," she said with the patience required to watch snow melt, "go rub down some horses, take a vacation, or write a book. Limpy will be here when Limpy gets here."

"Josie Cramer is dead," John said.

"What? Josie? How in the name of heaven!"

"I'm at her house now."

"Josie's dead?"

"Limpy needs to get over here right away."

"You wait there, John. I'll go over and see if I can breathe some life into him."

Limpy Logan was a sixty-year-old bachelor who exerted himself only to the extent required for coping with the rigors of a world that to him was a total mystery. He avoided women like smallpox, along with their demands for him to do all the things he spent a lifetime finding excuses for not doing. Observing what he called the deplorable behavior of children young and old, that any such person should ever call him daddy was beyond the realm of fantasy.

When County Sheriff Art Hicks asked Limpy if he wanted to be his deputy, Limpy declined the opportunity because he viewed it as an impediment to his freedom to go where he wanted, and do what he wanted when he wanted. But, Hicks, having exhausted his list of other possible candidates for the job, persuaded Limpy to pin on the deputy's badge with the promise that he wouldn't have to do anything. After all, in Blessing there had been no crime since Bonnie and Clyde. And, sad to say, Limpy dangled at the frazzled end of Hicks's official rope.

The phrase "wouldn't have to do anything" never made its way past Limpy's hearing organ. It stuck there like a walnut in a jaybird's craw. To Limpy it sounded like he wouldn't have to exert any effort and he'd get paid twenty-seven dollars a week for not doing it.

Hicks also promised "if the crime rate in Blessing decreases," Limpy would be in line for a raise in pay. The logic of the promise floated right over Logan's head. With no crime in Blessing, how could the crime rate decrease? Even so, he succumbed to the temptation of getting paid for doing nothing, for which he could have won the Pulitzer. For seven years after Limpy was installed as deputy sheriff of Blessing, the crime rate remained static—as in nonexistent—and Limpy was still waiting for the raise.

The "Limpy" label was pinned on Logan when Mrs. Clancy called him to replace a light bulb in the upstairs clothes closet of her boarding house. After wrestling for half an hour to get the old bulb out and a new one screwed in, Logan missed a step on his way out, tumbled down the stairs, and banged up a knee. The knee got gimpy, and ever since, no one called him Prudence, the name with which his mother saddled him at birth, retribution for his not being the hoped-for daughter.

Whatever Limpy knew about law enforcement he learned from his night watchman father, whose job years ago was patroling Blessing's downtown business places on foot. Making the rounds with his over-sized flashlight took eight minutes, a few minutes longer if he stopped at Si's for coffee.

A night watchman's responsibility was to check the store fronts to be sure they hadn't been tampered with. If he found one was tampered with, he was to call the sheriff's office. Only once during the years the security of Blessing was entrusted to the elder Logan did the sheriff make even a routine check of his efforts to protect the city of Blessing.

That was the night the sheriff found Limpy's father asleep by the front door of Mulhaney's Hardware. Toed awake by the sheriff, the elder Logan, still half asleep, didn't know where he was. With glazed eyes and flailing arms, he shouted, "Where's my boy?"

The sheriff relieved him of his flashlight, the cherished badge of a night watchman, affording Limpy's father ample time to search for his son.

In seven years as "the law" in Blessing, the most heart rending case Limpy was called upon to investigate was when Elsie McCloud frantically sought his assistance in locating her prized Persian tabby she hadn't seen for three days.

Limpy waged a search and found Elsie's cat under her front porch steps nursing a littler of six kittens. Elsie, appalled, bawled. "I'm not ready to be a grandmother!" she wailed.

Elsie was eighty-four. She died a year later and left all her cats to Goodwill.

Suddenly plunged into the middle of a murder investigation was something, if he thought of it at all, Limpy hoped he'd never be. He considered calling for help from Sheriff Hicks, but he rationalized that Arthur kept so busy out in the county, taking care of cattle thieves and beehive robbers, Limpy decided against it. Besides, if he could solve Josie's murder without the sheriff's help, he might qualify for the raise he was promised and never got.

How to go about investigating a murder to Limpy was as confusing as a flaming comet.

Yet, here he stood, pleading eyes focused on John Willingham, cringing at the sight of the lifeless body of Josie Cramer, seeking answers to questions he hardly knew how to ask.

"Who do you reckon coulda done it?" Limpy said to John.

"I'll tell you what, sheriff," John said with an effort to put a lid on his exasperation, "if I had any idea who did it, I'd be out there looking for him, instead of sitting around jawing with you."

"Now, now, Mr. Willingham, if I was you, I wouldn't be going off on no tangent. That won't do no good toward finding out who killed Josie—

Cramer, was it?"

"Maybe if you took a look around, you might find some fingerprints or some kind of evidence that would do some good."

The deputy stared at him over the tops of his wire-rimmed spectacles. At that moment it occurred to Limpy that he'd never before got a good look at John Willingham. Of course, there was that time at the Welcome Back Bar & Grill when John got involved in some kind of fracas, and Limpy gave him a lift home. At no other time could he recall exchanging a word with John, aside from an occasional howdy at Si's or the Post Office.

Limpy didn't think John looked like a killer. But, from what he read in those detective magazines, most killers didn't look like killers. Some of them were Sunday school teachers. He even read once about a high school drummer who beat somebody to death with her drumsticks, and they let her go, ruling it self-defense. The drummer didn't look like a killer either, besides which she was the only drummer they had.

Limpy knew John's daddy. Kyle was a good man, even if he did take off without telling anybody where he was going.

But you couldn't always tell by what their daddy was like. Look at Al Capone. Limpy read some place that Al's daddy went to mass twice a day, and look what happened to his boy.

You never know, do you? Limpy counseled himself in silent meditation. You just never know.

"Where was you?" he said to John, "between six and seven o'clock tonight?"

John glared at him, startled that Limpy even thought to ask where he was when the murder took place. After he found Josie's body, the first thing John did was to get on the phone and call Logan. It never occurred to him he might be the prime suspect.

When Limpy finally showed up at Josie's, he viewed the body from her bedroom door. Visibly shaken, he announced, "She's dead," which John already knew.

Limpy decided, and shared the wisdom with Wiilingham, maybe he should call Seth Gibbs to remove the body to the funeral home.

When Gibbs showed up, Limpy said to Seth, "She's dead."

Gibbs gave him a tolerant "I know" look, covered the body with a white sheet, and wheeled it out on a gurney.

Again Limpy said to John, "Where was you between six and seven o'clock tonight?" With Sherlock intensity he looked John squarely in the eyes. "Near as I can tell, that's when Josie— Cramer, was it?—was killed."

"Why do you think that?" John said.

Limpy peered over the tops of his wire rims again.

"Us lawmen have ways of tellin'," he said, as if to elaborate would betray the sanctity of the code.

John gave his head what he thought was a patient nod, but it didn't come off that way.

"Do you think I did it?" he said.

"Well, now, Mr. Willingham—"

"Do you think I killed Josie?"

"Well, you was the one that found her, Mr. Willingham," Limpy whined. "Everybody knows you and her was keeping company. Looks to me like you was the last one to see her alive. How'd I know mebby you done it, then mebby you reported it so's it would look like you never done it?" The left side of Limpy's mouth drooped into an accusing sag. "Happens all the time. And you ain't told me yet where you was between six and seven o'clock tonight."

"I was on my way here," John said, drawing on what was left of his patience. "I started walking from home about six o'clock. Dude Martin picked me up and brought me into town. He'll tell you that."

"How come you was walking?"

"Well–uh–Mama and I had a little disagreement, and I just took off. I've walked it before."

"How long does it take you to get to town from your place?"

"It's about a ten minute ride. Big end of an hour on foot."

"And you rode in with who?"

"Dude Martin."

"Uh-huh. Dude hauled you in, did he? Is he still driving that old Chevy truck with the rusted fenders?"

It was a stretch for John to make a connection between Dude's rusted Chevy truck fenders and the murder of Josie Cramer.

"Dude brought you here, did he?" Limpy said.

"No. He dropped me off at the Welcome

Back."

Limpy's slit-eyed squint told John that mention of the evil honky-tonk changed the complexion of the situation. Limpy got suspicious. Nothing good ever came out of the Welcome Back Bar & Grill. They danced and drank booze and smoked them filthy cigarettes, and no telling what else took place in that den of iniquity.

"What was you doing at the honky-tonk?" Limpy said, viewing the suspect with a piercing eye.

"I stopped by there to get a couple of hamburgers."

"For who?"

"I was on my way here to see Josie, so I brought the burgers for her and me."

"How long was you there—at the honky tonk?"

"It's hard to say," John said. "They're pretty busy at that time on Sunday."

"Anybody see you?"

"Lena Bradley."

"Lena was there, was she?"

"Lena is always there. And I talked to Ernie Phipps for a few minutes."

"What was Ernie doing there?"

"He was having some kind of sandwich and a beer."

"Did you have anything to drink—mebby a little nip or two while you was waiting for—burgers, was it?"

"I didn't have anything to drink."

"Uh-huh." Limpy was having a hard time finding questions to ask. "Mebby you got likkered up while you was waiting at the honky-tonk, then mebby you and her had a tiff over something or other, and mebby you was taking it out on her—whatever it was you and your mama was at it about. Then mebby you got so riled up you choked her till her neck was broke."

John fought the urge to throttle the deputy, but decided against it. Inept as he was, Limpy Logan was only trying to do what he perceived was his job.

"Look, sheriff, Josie and I were good friends. I know some people didn't think it was right we spent time together, but she was a good person. I don't know why anybody would want to see her dead."

Logan's little black eyes narrowed into slits. He stared at John, dead certain he had cornered the culprit red-handed. Lots of killers—like the ones in them magazines—talked about how good the ones was that they knifed in the heart. Trying to throw you off guard, like they wasn't no way they could'a done such a vile deed.

John said, "Would you have wanted her dead?"

"Hup! Now, Mr. Willingham—"

"Where were you between six and seven tonight?"

"Now, I don't think we need to—"

"You see, sheriff. It looks different from the other side, doesn't it?"

"Mebby I was a little quick on the trigger. Us lawmen do that sometimes when we need to find out who done something or other. Mebby you didn't do it."

"You know I didn't do it."

"But I'm locking you up anyhow."

"What!"

"You're all I got to go on. That woman's laying over there in Seth Gibbs's funeral parlor deader'n a rock, and I got no idy why, unless it's because you put her there. So, till I find out something different, you're gonna be eating on county money."

"Now, hold on, sheriff. Are you charging me?"

"With the murder—the brutal, brutal murder of Miss Josie–Cramer, was it?"

"You know damn well who she was! You were over there sniffing around at her place often enough."

"Hup!" Logan hupped, pointing an admonishing finger. "Now, Mr. Willingham, my visits to Miss—"

"Josie Cramer."

"Whenever I paid her a call it was strictly official business."

"Uh-huh. She told me she saw you snooping around outside her window at night."

"Hup! Snooping? Snooping?"

"That's what she called it."

"I was just doing my job. I heard she was afraid of prowlers. It's what us lawmen call undercover."

John couldn't believe it. This man, bungler though he was, still represented the law in Blessing. He began to view Limpy in a different light. There was nobody else he could nail for Josie's murder, and this scrawny little sad excuse for a deputy sheriff could throw him in jail, guilty or not. And that was what he had in mind!

"Look, sheriff," John said, "we both know I

didn't kill Josie. I wasn't anywhere near here when you say the murder took place."

Limpy stretched to his full five-and-a-half-foot height, assumed what he considered to be an authoritative expression, and in his most officious tone of voice proclaimed, "John Willingham, I'm arresting you for the murder of Josie—Cramer, was it?"

Nobody could remember the last time there was a murder in Blessing, Oklahoma. Now, news of Josie's death spread like chaff in a whirlwind. It created a wave of fear among the citizenry, complacent as they usually were that nothing disturbed their uneventful comings and goings.

The Parker sisters locked and barred their doors and windows against an attack by what they were positive was a vicious killer—right after they called Clara and told her "that woman" was dead.

"We knew you'd want to know," they told her.

Clara's hand shook so at the foreboding news she almost dropped the phone.

"Did you see anybody go in there?" Clara said through trembling lips.

No, the sisters said, they were at church at the time, but news of the murder was "all over town."

Clara breathed more easily, relieved that neither she nor John was seen going into, nor out of, Josie's bungalow. She dropped the phone into its cradle and pressed her sweaty palms against her thighs.

She was afraid for John.

From the lips of the shocked citizenry rose the

question: Who killed the whore?

Limpy spread the word that John Willingham found her body, and was the last person to see Josie alive, making him the obvious suspect. Even so, in the end, Limpy released John on his own "recognizance" while he investigated further, partly because the jail wouldn't hold anybody since the lock on the cell door was rusted open for lack of use, but mostly because Limpy didn't know what else to do with him. He even gave John a ride home again.

John's friends, except for Dude Martin, were adamant in their support.

When Dude was interviewed by a TV news crew out of Tulsa, he told them of a time or two when he recalled seeing John "fly off the handle," as if he was not ready to bear witness to John's innocence.

"I'm just bein' square about it," Dude said with a dour expression when somebody challenged his years long friendship with his neighbor.

The Monday morning decaf and donuts crowd at Dixie's Do Drop Inn was abuzz with speculation as to who killed the woman who was guilty of nothing more than minding her own business.

"Damn shame!" said Cody Willis.

Cody was nineteen months past retirement from the Post Office and couldn't hear much of anything, but he talked loud.

"Damn shame!" Cody said again, cupping an ear with his hand to be sure he said what he meant to.

"Who'd want to do an outlandish thing like

that?" Rufus put in.

Dixie, thin and graying, poured another round of coffee.

"Find that out," she said, "and you've got yourself a killer."

"I'd never believe John Willingham done it," Rufus said.

"John never done it!" Ernie put in.

"Well, I don't know," Skelly Wilks said, and he really didn't.

"No, you don't know," Cody piped up. "Nobody knows, except the one that done it. But if I had any betting money, I'd put it all down that it wasn't John Willingham."

"That girl," said Dixie, making the rounds with her Silex coffee pot, "deserved a lot better than what she got."

"Damn sure did!" Cody agreed.

Skelly nodded his agreement. He held out his cup for a refill, and dumped in another spoonful of sugar.

"Biggest thing ever happened in this town," he said.

"Everybody in town is so common and close," Rufus said. "Why, I mind the time when we didn't even have a deputy, because we all took care of each other."

"Never needed one till now," Ernie said.

"And where was he when we needed him?" Rufus wanted to know.

"Same place he is right now, I'd judge," Cody said.

Around the table heads nodded and shook

derisively, shoulders shrugged, and hands spread wide. Everybody had a notion where Limpy was.

Home in bed.

CHAPTER 11

John makes a decision

Monday morning John woke up with a head full of questions about what took place the night before. Heading for the field, he needed time to work things out in his mind. Over and over he asked himself what happened to Josie. Somebody drove the Pontiac last night, and he had trouble believing his mother was at the wheel, since she was a nervous wreck with the thought of driving anyplace by herself. Had she somehow maneuvered the Pontiac out of the shed and onto the road, and paid Josie a visit? If so—

His mother's volatile tongue and explosive temper could erupt at any moment without warning. But was she—his mother!—capable of committing murder? Even in a roaring rage, red-in-the-face positive Josie was corrupting her son, could she take the life of another human being—somebody she didn't even know? John tried to deny the answer forcing its way to the forefront of his mind.

If Clara weren't his mother, would the answer come more easily?

John discovered his old red bull had ripped another hole in the garden fence. He rounded up the bull, got him back in the pasture, and repaired the fence. Simple. Over and done with. All it took was a little time, and a dab of the elbow grease his mother told him about. He wished for as simple a solution to the problem nagging at him like a throbbing boil. Josie was dead, and he struggled with the possibility that his mother killed her.

After Limpy dropped him off last night, John noticed the front end of the Pontiac was sticking out of the shed, and the hood was still warm. Why had the car been moved? He grudgingly convinced himself that Clara was the only person who would have driven it, and he needed to know to where, when, and why.

At lunch time Monday, Clara placed his food on the table, humbly as a worshipful slave. She knew what he would talk about when the time came for talk, and didn't look forward to it. Her brain was in a whirl, trying to work out what she would say when John told her Josie was dead, as she knew he would.

"Mama, Josie's dead."

His words wracked her body with cold shivers. She almost dropped the coffee pot when she refilled his cup.

Sometime during last night she heard the front door squeak open. Rarely could she sleep before

John got home from wherever he went. She tossed about, wondering when, or if, he would be back home that night. The squeaking door signaled that she could safely drop off to sleep. John was home, and she did.

Still asleep when he left for the field Monday morning, she hadn't seen him since he left for town the night before. But now, here he was at the table, ignoring his favorite pork chops and mashed potatoes drowned in cream gravy, telling her what she already knew from the sisters' call.

"Josie Cramer is dead."

Clara couldn't believe it when they told her either. And to hear the same words from the mouth of her son was almost unbearable.

After the sisters called, Clara had no idea she might be a suspect in Josie's death, but now she wasn't sure. Yes, she was angry with Josie, angry enough to shove her against the chiffarobe. But that was all.

Josie was alive when she left her. But, now how sure was she?

"Limpy Logan thinks I killed Josie," John said, "because he says I was the last person to see her alive."

Clara covered her mouth with a nervous hand.

"You, son? Why, you couldn't—" She choked on the words.

John decided the best way to say it was straight out.

"Where did you go in the car last night, Mama?"

"The car?"

"The motor was still warm when I got home."

"Why, I—"

"Limpy thinks Josie died between six and seven o'clock last night." He stared into her fright filled eyes. "Did you go see Josie last night, Mama?"

"Well, I just—you know—I—"

Ashen faced, she could hardly hold the coffee pot with her shaking hands.

"Did you kill Josie, Mama?"

"Kill her?" she flared. "You think I'd kill that little whore? I hated her for what she was doing to you, but—"

"Did you kill Josie, Mama?"

"That's right! Blame your poor old mother. Anything that goes wrong around here is my fault! Just like that man who ran off and left us. He blamed me for everything too." She plopped onto a chair. Her body convulsed. "You think I don't know what that woman was doing to you? You think I could stand by and let her ruin your life? I didn't go to hurt her, but I went there to make sure she didn't hurt you anymore."

John felt the strength draining from his body. He was fighting with his heart against what logic was forcing him to see. He hoped Clara had a reasonable explanation for why she took the car when she hardly knew how to drive. He wanted her to tell him she went to the store, to church, to visit a friend. Any place but to see Josie Cramer.

She couldn't have been with Josie for more than a few minutes, no longer than it took John to stop at the Welcome Back, pick up the hamburgers, and walk to Josie's. The way it played out in his mind, he could see Clara, red-faced, abusive, letting Josie know she didn't approve of her relationship with John. Shocked, Josie probably protested, and Clara attacked her in a blind fury.

Fearing his mother, not he, was the last person to see Josie alive, John had to make a decision. Should he turn her over to Limpy Logan? Could he let Arthur Hicks lock her in his jail, where she would go out of her mind in a week? She'd be forced to wither for God only knew how long? On what charge? Premeditated murder? His mother?

Clara slumped against the table, wiping tears on her apron.

"Mama," John said in a calm voice, "don't go any place, don't answer the phone, and don't tell anybody what we talked about."

"You think I killed her, John?" she said through trembling lips.

"I don't know, Mama. I don't know. I hope not."

His mind was made up. He knew what he had to do.

Hamp visits Simon

Simon Colby settled into his leather recliner with holes worn in the arms, sipping at his coffee. His mind was as muddled as a bucketful of centipedes. Josie's murder was load enough to carry for one day. But now, sitting there, looking at him with a Cheshire cat grin on his face was the man he'd swear Seth Gibbs put in the ground two years ago. Skelly Wilks told him Hamp Hargrove was alive. What Skelly said wasn't always reliable, but Rufus put a good deal of stock in whatever the mayor told him. Simon bunched Rufus and Skelly together with the crowd at Dixie's, slurping coffee, trying to figure out who killed Josie Cramer.

None of them knew anything, but Simon did. Simon knew John Williingham didn't do it. He'd swear to it on a mile-high stack of the King James Version, without any more proof than anyone else had/ that John Willingham did not kill Josie Cramer. Simon knew in his heart John would never be guilty of killing anyone—drunk, out of his mind, or with the muzzle of a shotgun nudging his nose.

Si thought his seventy-seven-year-old eyes were playing tricks on him, asking him to believe it was Hamp Hargrove's bulk draped over his wooden stool next to the meat counter. Hamp was trying to convince him he wasn't in the box Seth lowered into a grave in the Baptist Church cemetery two years ago. After his encounter with the one-armed giant, Ernie told Simon he was pretty sure Hamp was alive, since he stood there looking at Hargrove's blood shot eyes. Si believed Ernie, but it was still a tough pill to swallow.

"They paid me a visit one night," Si heard Hargrove saying.

"Who's they?" Si asked.

"A couple of gun toters from Kansas City. There was some shooting going on. I got hit and fell over in my front yard and stayed down. The one that done the shooting was across the road from my place. He must've thought I was done for, and didn't shoot no more.

"I was hurt bad, I'll give you that. Somehow I was able to crawl to the back door of Seth's funeral parlor. He took me in and fixed me up the best he could. I told Seth what happened and— I didn't want them guys coming back. Seth and me, we made it up I'd pay him for the box, but he'd bury a bunch of logs instead of me.

"He put out the word I was in too bad shape to open the casket."

"I recollect that," Simon said.

"I didn't want anybody to know I was alive," Hamp said. "I was afraid they might come back and finish the job. Seth drove me over to Muskogee, and put me on a bus to Arkansas. Nobody knew the difference till I come back a week ago."

Si shook his head in disbelief.

"What about them other fellers?" he said. "The ones that done the shootin'."

"Dead. They're all dead, or in the pen. There ain't nobody after me now. That's why I come back."

"Why did they come after you?"

Hargrove glanced around to satisfy himself that he and Si were the only ones listening.

"In a Kansas City bar one night, I got into a tussle with a young drunk guy, and he pulled a knife on me. I knocked him against the bar, and he hit his head on it when he fell.

"He wasn't bad hurt, but it turned out his daddy was some kind of big-time crime boss. I guess he didn't like me beating up on his boy, so he sent them guys after me."

"I'da swore you was in that box that Seth

113

buried." Si gave his head a bewildered shake. "You say you been in Arkansas all this time?"

Hargrove nodded. "A cousin of mine put me up. It took quite a while for me to get back on my feet. When I did, I hired on with some people down there in the hog manufacturing business."

"Hog manufacturing?"

"That's what I call it. They buy up land in different parts of the country, and build these plants where they breed maybe twenty thousand hogs at a time, fatten them up, and ship 'em out to market."

"Twenty thousand hogs?"

"At one time."

"Don't that stir up a terrible stink?"

"Some folks think so. But," Hargrove said with a grin, "the kind of money they pay for land can make hog shit smell like roses."

"Is that what you've been talking to John Willingham about?"

"Him and some others. A few of the farmers talk like they're willing to sell out, but some others are pretty damn stubborn. One of the stubborn ones is Willingham. The hog people are stubborn too." He rubbed his chin with a folded fist. "We ain't tried everything yet."

"Skelly Wilks says you threatened to burn John's house down."

With a crooked grin, Hargrove said, "Like I said, we ain't tried everything yet."

"If I was you I wouldn't push Willingham too hard."

"We'll see. He's got something bigger pushing him right now."

"You mean that killing?" Si said.

"You think he done it?"

"I've known John all his life, and his daddy before him," Si said. "John wouldn't do a thing like that. I wouldn't be afraid to bet the Sak'n Pak on it."

Simon stared at the big man with no left arm, bewildered yet that it really was Hamp Hargrove he was talking to.

"You seen Dudley lately?" Si said.

Hamp was surprised by the question. "Dudley—?"

"Coe. Dudley Coe, the handyman."

Hargrove shook his head. "Not since I got back."

"If you run across him, tell him I've got a job of work he can do for me."

Hargrove nodded and got up to leave.

"I'll do that," he said.

Si said, "I guess you wasn't in that box, after all."

"I guess not."

CHAPTER 12

John Willingham comes to town

Loud, angry shouts jarred Limpy Logan awake from a sound sleep. He knuckled the sleep from his eyes, and rolled over in bed, half blinded by the bright daylight he hadn't seen for hours.

Who in tarnation was raising such a ruckus in his front yard at four o'clock on a Monday afternoon?

He crawled out of bed, fully clothed, and peeked over the front room window sill. His squinting eyes fell upon a gang of fist-shaking rabblerousers whose mamas never taught them to respect a man's privacy and need for rest.

The balding, rotund Reverend Clovis Groop, who condemned Josie and her money as unfit for the innocent members of his flock, was directing the fury Limpy was trying to figure out. More than thirty of Groop's wrought up disciples traipsed with him the seven miles from Springer to Blessing. Their mission was to protest in the deputy's front yard because he "released upon the unsuspecting public a killer to kill again!"

Whipped into a frenzy by the fiery-voiced Groop, the mob shook their fists at Limpy's door, shouting demands for the killer's arrest.

"In the name of the Lord God Almighty," Groop screamed at Limpy's front door, "arrest that killer and bring him to justice!"

Limpy thought ever so briefly about going out there and facing the mob to complain about their trampling what was left of the grass in his front yard. While he was thinking about it, he heard Louise yell at him out her window. He knew Louise wouldn't disturb his rest, except for something really big. On his hands and knees he made his way to his window and yanked the cord on the shade that rattled all the way up, shattering his nerves.

"Are you up, sheriff?" Louise said when she saw the shade fly up, lamenting still the day she was unlucky enough to find a vacant house to rent next door.

Limpy waved a hand, a signal he hadn't died in his sleep.

"You better get out there and do something," Louise admonished in a voice that gave Limpy the shivers, "before those people tear your house down."

"What do they want?" he croaked.

"Go find out!" Louise slammed the window down.

The deputy stumbled to the front door, opened

it a crack, and peeked out.

A riled up protester with tousled hair hanging to his waist spotted Limpy in the crack of the door. "Behold! Our illustrious champion of the law!" the protester proclaimed derisively.

The crowd chorused, "Arrest that killer and bring him to justice."

After a moment's consideration, Limpy decided he could do one of two things: He could go out there and risk being torn limb from limb by a bunch of crazy people dead set on forcing him to do something that he didn't know how to do, or he could slam his door shut, throw the deadlock, and go back to bed.

The second choice was the one he liked best, but Louise screamed at him in no uncertain terms to "do something."

He eased the door open a bit wider and peered out. Could he set foot on his own front porch and live to talk about it? Limpy was saved by the sound of a blaring siren headed toward his house. Arthur Hicks's cruiser careened around the corner, and skidded to a stop near the collection of irate protesters.

Hicks unwound from the cruiser, and slammed the door behind him, scanning the crowd that his arrival reduced to silence. Hicks recognized Groop as a rabid activist, the preacher who, a few weeks before, waged an unsuccessful campaign to close all the "dens of iniquity" in the county, including bowling alleys, pool halls, and bars, along with dance halls and restaurants that served beer.

"Workshops of the devil!" Groop shouted from

the courthouse steps. He also staged sit-ins, blocking the doors of such unsavory establishments as the Welcome Back Bar & Grill.

Lena Bradley put in a frantic call to Sheriff Hicks. Hicks had arrived in his siren-blasting cruiser and removed the protesters with the threat of arrest.

Except for a glimpse out the corner of his eye, the sheriff paid the preacher no mind, striding to Limpy's front door. The deputy stood transfixed, with the hope that Hicks's presence would defer his demise.

"What the hell's going on here, Logan?" Hicks said in a low voice.

Before Limpy could work up an answer he hoped would make sense to the county sheriff, the mob chanted, "Where's John Willingham, where's John Willingham, where's John Willingham?"

To Logan, Hicks said, "Where's John Willingham?"

"At home I reckon," Limpy said in a barely audible voice. "I let him go till I could—"

"You let him go?"

"—get something solid on him."

"You're not authorized to make that decision, Logan. Why didn't you call me right away, instead of waiting for me to hear about this on the radio?"

"Figgered you was too busy."

Hicks gave his head an incredulous shake.

"Let's go pick him up," he said, moving toward the cruiser.

To the crowd, he said, "You people go on back to wherever you came from. This is police business, and is none of your concern."

"Where's the killer?" Groop shouted. He wasn't ready to give up, leading his charges in a sneering chant, "Kill the killer, kill the killer, kill the killer!"

Hicks ignored them, and motioned Logan to follow him to the cruiser.

"If you don't, we will," Groop yelled, and his disciples echoed like a flock of parrots, "If you don't we will, if you don't we will, if you don't we will!"

Hicks tossed them a disgusted wave.

The protesters muttered their displeasure, and watched the black-and-white speed away with Hicks and Logan in it.

Herding his red Ford pickup south, half way to town, John caught sight of rotating lights and heard the wail of a siren speeding his way. It was Arthur Hicks, in a hurry to get some place. John had an idea where Hicks was headed. He pulled onto the shoulder and slowed to a stop, waiting for Hicks to come even on the other side of the road.

Hicks scattered gravel skidding to a stop. He couldn't believe he was sitting there looking at the man he was on his way to arrest for the murder of Josie Cramer.

"Is that you, John?" Hicks said.

"It's me, Art. I'm on my way to see Logan."

"Logan? Logan's with me." Hicks looked around to be sure Limpy was still there. "We're on our way to see you."

"Is it about Josie?" John said.

"Yeah."

"I guess I can save you the trouble."

"How's that, John?"

John spent a sleepless Sunday night, and most of Monday, sweating in the field, searching for a way to handle the matter of Josie's death without implicating his mother. Limpy told him he wouldn't lock him up after all because he hadn't had time to investigate, and had no "conducive evidence" that John was the guilty party.

Even so, John's decision was quite simple: To save his mother, he would turn himself in. "I guess I'm the one you're looking for," John said to Hicks.

Hicks's face clouded with confusion. The man he was on his way to arrest for murder met him half way to town? "Are you saying you killed Josie Cramer?"

"Limpy must've told you—he's got the goods on me."

"Well—"

That was not what the sheriff expected to hear. He knew John as an honorable, peace loving man. But he was the law, and John was his only suspect, so he felt the need to do something official.

"Well, I guess I'll have to take you in, John."

"I guess so, Art."

"You want to follow me?"

John nodded. "I already told Mama where I'd be."

"Clara knows about this?"

"I told her. I'm ready, Art. Let's get it done."

John would have bet his mother's farm he

would never see the inside of a jail unless he was visiting somebody there, which he never did. He didn't know anybody who was ever in jail.

When Hicks slammed that heavy metal door shut behind him with an ear-shattering clang, John learned in a hurry what being locked in a cage felt like. Surrounded by walls of concrete, steel bars separating him from the outside world, he felt what would upset a cornered rat, looking for a way out.

Wrapped in a blanket of lonesome, John recalled the cold, wet night he arrived at Fort Sill to volunteer for the army as a country kid from Blessing. Along with dozens of other raw recruits, crammed shoulder to shoulder in a troop truck, he wished he had been doing something else when he decided to join up. If there was a hill to go over, he was homesick enough to try it.

But there was no hill, and he was helpless as a 'possum with a foot in a trap. Like it or not, cold and wet as it was, he was in the army, and after the homesickness wore off, he was glad he didn't try to escape. That was a long time ago, and back then there were no clanging doors and steel bars penning him in.

News of Josie's death arrived at the jail before John did. The jaundiced eyes of glaring strangers checked him over. At least one of them pegged him guilty without a trial.

John didn't know who killed Josie, and didn't like where his suspicions took him, but he was next to certain Clara had something to do with it, and didn't hesitate to shift the blame to himself. To save his mother, he'd stand up to whatever the law threw at him, glaring jail cell strangers and all.

There were three other prisoners in the cell where Hicks slammed that steel door behind him.

The youngest of the three was Jason Baird. Jason was a sullen seventeen-year-old awaiting trial for assaulting a loud bad-mouther of the home team at a high school baseball game. Light haired and fair skinned, Jason's brooding brown eyes revealed no emotion. He regarded with passive interest the arrival of a new cell mate, and went back to dealing solitaire on his top bunk.

Luther Gaston had stringy blond hair, with a scraggly beard and mustache. He was serving time for breaking and entering.

Gaston wasted no time with his needling John about Josie's murder.

"So, you're the whore killer?" Gaston said with a smirk.

The best John could muster in response was a tolerant look.

"Ain't talking, eh, old man?" Gaston jeered. "Big tough woman killer."

The third man in the cell, a few years older than John, called himself Jimmy Pleasant. John silently bet Jimmy Pleasant wasn't the name his mother gave him when she pushed him out of her stomach. He would learn Pleasant adopted the name to fit his image as a country singer.

Pleasant learned to pick a guitar before he could carry a tune. Like other pickers and grinners, his lifelong dream was to grace the stage of the Grand Ole Opry along with such stars as Earnest Tubb, Red Foley, and Webb Pierce. He'd tell you he was good enough to "make it," even as good as those guys, but he wasn't as successful as Eddy Arnold and Porter Wagoner because "they got the breaks" and he didn't.

At forty-one, Pleasant believed his dream of "making it big" would one day still come true. That was, until he got himself busted for dealing drugs. Stardom for Jimmy would have to wait. He was convicted in Judge Herman Yokum's court, and was awaiting transfer to prison where he'd serve six years. Jimmy's gray-streaked brown hair lapped over his collar, and his red face showed signs of spending time trying to liberate Johnny Walker from the bottom of a bottle.

"He ain't talking about the whore killing," Gaston said to Pleasant. "Maybe we ought to have our own little trial right here."

"Don't make a shit to me, Luther," Pleasant said.

"You better be talking to somebody, old man," Gaston said to John, "or your ass will go to seed in here."

Two bunks were stacked against each of two cell walls, and John stretched out on the bottom of one of them.

"That's my bunk," Gaston said.

"I don't see your name on it," John said.

"Don't need no name on it, man. That's where I sleep."

Pleasant watched with little interest to see where the dispute was going. He knew Gaston was a short-fused hothead who could explode like a cherry bomb, and he half expected it to happen.

The Baird boy looked up from his card game. He couldn't care less one way or the other. The challenge was only something different from the boredom of a day when nothing happened.

John crawled off the bunk, and climbed onto the one above it without a word.

Gaston kept at him."You ain't got a lot of fire in your belly, have you, old man? I guess it don't take much to kill a whore."

John pinned him with a stare. "How old are you, Luther?" he asked.

"Twenty-four, if it's any of your business. Why?"

"I just wondered how long it took you to be such an asshole."

"You got a big mouth, man!" Luther made a threatening move toward John.

"Knock it off, Luther," Pleasant said. "What he thinks don't make a shit. You'll be out of here in a few weeks."

Gaston backed off with fire in his eyes.

Willingham turned his face to the wall. Gaston was the least of his worries. Pleasant was wrong about Gaston. He would never breathe free air again.

CHAPTER 13

Let's get 'er done

Why the wheels of justice turned so slowly John Willingham had no notion. With nothing to look forward to, except more of what was depriving him of freedom, caged like a lion behind gray walls and steel bars, the days crept by slowly as a snail in cold sorghum.

John lost count of how many days passed since Arthur Hicks locked him in his jail. His mother's daily visits became so stressful she "couldn't take it anymore." Depressed and downhearted, Clara felt she was doing more harm than good by showing up to visit her son in jail. Things to talk about hid behind a cloud of suspicion and uncertainty. John was glad Clara limited her visits to two times a week.

Lawyer Charlie Bates dropped by to find out if John remembered anything more he should know about. Guards from the state pen showed up one day and hauled Jimmy Pleasant away in handcuffs and leg irons. John wished him luck as he left.

The Baird boy was sent home, sentenced to time served.

Gaston calmed down. Dumb and thick headed as Luther was, with only a few more weeks to serve, he didn't want to do anything to tack more time onto his sentence.

But he would.

"I'll have to keep you locked up for a while, John," Hicks said when he brought John in.

"How long?" John wanted to know. Depends on how fast they move on it. It's up to them now."

"Who is, they?"

"The prosecutor mostly. That's Will Starkey. He'll have to make an investigation to find out if there's probable cause to bring charges. If so, there'll be an arraignment. Then, if it comes to trial, the judge will have to find room for it on the docket."

"How long does that take?"

"Well, I hear Starkey made plans for an African safari, so he could ask the judge to step it up a little. Or he could ask for a delay. No telling what they'll work out till it's done."

Hicks hung his head and scratched his nose.

"I'm sorry to do this to you, John. It's my job."

"I know. That's all right, Art."

"I've got to tell you, you're the last man in the county I thought I'd ever be slamming this door on."

"It's okay, Art. Like you say, it's your job."

"I might could get you out on bail, if you'd go

for that"

"No. I'll be fine. Let's get on with it."

Benny Pelham came by a few times, representing the press. He knelt on the floor outside John's cell and talked to him through the bars. Benny made notes on a yellow writing pad balanced on his knee. Benny didn't do much writing, though. John figured he was the first murder suspect the young newspaperman ever interviewed.

"Did you kill Josie?" Benny said.

John had a ready answer for that.

"Go ask Limpy Logan." He wished he could come up with some startling news to share with the young editor, but couldn't think of any.

Charlie Bates was seven years old when his father, an off-duty policeman, was convicted and served time for helping friends rob the bank he was paid to protect as a night guard.

Charlie endured the taunts of his school mates—"robber's kid, robber's kid, ain't you sorry that he did?" Humiliated and embarrassed, Charlie cried tears that his mother's hugs couldn't dry. Even so, by the time he finished high school, Charlie made up his mind he wasn't going to allow his life to be characterized by the stigma of his father's crime. Instead, he earned a law degree from Oklahoma State, and used his father's conviction as a springboard to a successful career in legal defense.

Willingham told Sheriff Hicks he didn't need a lawyer. Hicks said he did, and recommended Charlie Bates. Bates, a barrel chested, no nonsense practitioner, earned the respect of his peers as a tenacious defender of the law.

Bates's first question when he interviewed John at the jail was, "Did you kill Josie Cramer?"

Pelham asked the same question. The difference was Charlie was looking for something on which to build a case in John's defense, while Benny wanted a story to sell some copies of the Blessing Blessing.

John had no answer for Bates. He lowered his eyes and said nothing.

"You want to tell me what happened?" Charlie said.

"Where do I start?"

"What time did you leave home?"

"I'd say it was around six thirty. I was on my way to town when Dude Martin picked me up and gave me a ride to town."

"You were walking to town?"

"Yes. I've done it before."

"Who is Dude Martin?"

"A neighbor. He farms the place south of me."

Bates wrote something on a blue-lined note pad.

"I asked Dude to let me off at the Welcome Back," John said.

"What's the Welcome Back?"

"It's a local hangout. They sell beer and sandwiches. I stopped there to pick up a couple of hamburgers for supper."

"For whom?"

"Josie and me."

Bates scribbled more notes as John talked.

"I had a beer while I waited," John said,

recalling Limpy's speculation of how he spent time at the Welcome Back while Lena fried the burgers.

"You had a beer?" Charlie said.

"Well, maybe more than I thought."

"Who saw you at the Welcome Back?"

"Lena Bradley, the bartender."

"Anyone else?"

"Ernie Phipps. I talked to Ernie a little bit."

"Phipps. You spell that with a PH?"

John nodded.

"What did you talk to Ernie about?"

"An outfit in Arkansas wants to buy up land around here for a hog operation. Ernie works at the packing plant. I thought he might have heard something I didn't know—what other farmers were saying about that."

"Go ahead."

"When I got to Josie's we disagreed about something—I don't remember what. Sometimes when I drink I get a little crazy, and I—"

"You what?"

"I never meant to hurt her."

"Did you kill Josie Cramer?"

"I think you know the answer to that."

"That's not what I asked you, John. Did you kill Josie Cramer?"

"We're wasting time, Charlie."

Bates wasn't satisfied with what he heard. Most people he defended couldn't protest their innocence loudly enough, yet here was a man who, for reasons Charlie didn't know, and was trying to find out, knocking himself out to convince his lawyer he committed murder. "What time did you get to

Josie's house?" Charlie asked.

"It's hard to say. I don't know how long I was at the Welcome Back."

Bates gave his head a bewildered shake. "John, are you telling me the truth? I can't help you if you don't tell me exactly what happened?"

"Come on, Charlie——-"

"Dammit, man, I'm trying to save your life! Why do you want me to believe you killed that woman?"

"Facts are facts."

"Well, I don't think I've heard the facts. Was Josie alive when you got there?"

"What are you trying to prove, Charlie?"

"I'm trying to disprove what you're working so hard to get me to believe, and I don't understand why."

"Well, Charlie, you're a good lawyer. You probably don't remember the last time you lost a case. And I bet there's nothing in those law books of yours that says you have to understand."

Bates stared at him, trying to penetrate the enigmatic expression plastered on the face of John Willingham. "Do you realize what you're up against here?" Bates expected no response, and got none. "A woman is dead—a woman with whom you had a close relationship for—what, a year or two?"

"That's about right. Couple of years."

"Sheriff Hicks says you were the last person to see her alive."

John made no comment. Charlie was telling him things he already knew. Why couldn't they just get on with it, whatever it was?

"Your fingerprints were found all over the place," Bates went on.

That was no surprise to John. He was in Josie's home many times in the two years he knew her.

"The prosecutor has issued a criminal complaint against you," Bates said. "That means you could be tried for murder. If convicted, you could be sentenced to death. Do you understand what I'm saying?"

John thought about that. "I understand there'll be a hearing."

"Yes, after which it'll be determined whether you're eligible for bail. We'll go over all this before your court appearance. That'll be set by the judge, according to how full his docket is. Everything takes time, John."

"Sounds to me like a waste."

"You don't seem to realize your life may be at stake here."

John looked away, deep in thought.

"Ajax and elbow grease," he said.

"What does that mean?"

"My mother used to tell me Ajax and elbow grease can clean up about any kind of mess."

"Well, this is one mess that—"

"Forget it, Charlie. What's next?"

Bates shook his head. He fought the good fight and lost.

"If it gets that far," he said, "there'll be a trial, evidence presented and testimony by witnesses."

"Let's do that."

"One thing you need to remember, John. You won't have to go through this by yourself. I'll be on your side all the way. But my hands are tied unless I know what you know. The truth, the whole truth, and nothing but the truth, so help you God."

The arraignment set a record for brevity. Judge Herman P. Yokum looked at Prosecutor Will Starkey.

"The State versus John Willingham," the judge said.

"That's correct, Your Honor," Starkey said. "The charge is first degree murder."

Yokum looked at Charlie Bates. "How do you plead?"

"Not guilty, Your Honor."

No surprises there.

Herman P. recalled no suspect who ever pleaded guilty at arraignment. Even so, the law said a first degree murder charge remanded the defendant to jail to await trial. Herman so ruled. 'The court will hear the trial three Wednesdays from now." He pounded his gavel, pronounced the session over, and departed the premises.

CHAPTER 14

Herman's court"

All rise," the bailiff shouted. "The Honorable Herman P. Yokum presiding."

A noisy shuffling by the audience getting to its feet greeted the quick-step approach of the diminutive Judge Yokum. His black robe swirled around his ankles as he strode briskly to the bench, and seated himself in the huge leather bound chair behind the bench.

"Be seated," he said to the gallery.

Judge Yokum was sixty-four-years old, had sat on that bench for twenty-three years. In nine more months he'd reach his goal for retirement. He looked forward to fishing, boating on the lake with his grandson, and beating the boy's father at cribbage. Until then, however, he'd be a magistrate who got down to cases and disposed of them with fairness and justice.

Ignoring the gathering in the courtroom, Judge Yokum shuffled through some papers on the bench.

He finally got around to pounding the gavel, and his court was open for business. He peered over the tops of his black horn-rimmed glasses at the two lawyers seated at tables facing him. Charlie Bates, defense counsel, to his right, and Prosecutor Will Starkey on the left.

To the defendant's table, the judge said, "John Willingham."

He didn't know John Willingham, just as he didn't know any defendant who appeared in his court, whose future might well depend on his judgment. But he would hear John's case, just as he heard every case before, dispensing justice with honesty and fairness as prescribed by law.

John never saw Herman Yokum either until the moment Herman emerged from chambers behind the bench, but he thought the judge looked like a pretty decent fellow who would do what he could for him.

Starkey and Bates responded in unison, "That's correct, Your Honor."

Starkey grew up in a family of lawyers dating back to his great-grandfather on his mother's side. Will's dark eyes and sharp chin exemplified the determination with which he approached every case. For three years he served as assistant prosecutor under Cliff Wingert. Wingert drank himself to death and died of cirrhosis of the liver after nine years in office. Starkey succeeded him as prosecutor.

To Bates, the judge said, "You've entered a

plea of not guilty?"

"That's correct, Your Honor."

John frowned and clamped a protesting hand on Charlie's arm. Charlie shook it off.

To Starkey, the judge said, "You may proceed with your opening statement."

"If it pleases the Court," Starkey said, "the circumstances in this case are such that the State begs to forgo the opening statement and proceed to testimony."

"What are the circumstances?" Herman wanted to know.

"Your Honor, the accused has confessed to the charge, and I—"

"Objection!" Bates bounced out of his chair. "The accused has confessed to nothing, and just entered a plea of not guilty. I submit counsel is attempting to sway the jury before they've heard testimony."

"Sustained." To Starkey, Yokum said, "You want to proceed to testimony?"

"We do, Your Honor."

Yokum cast him a puzzled look, and shook his head. "I don't know what you're up to," he said, "but it's your ball game. Call your first witness."

"The State calls Deputy Sheriff Prudence Logan."

"Is Miss Logan in the courtroom?" Yokum glanced over the gallery.

At the back of the chamber the door swung open, and Limpy Logan was escorted to the witness box.

This was Prudence Logan?

The jurors hid smiles behind their hands. Most of them knew who the deputy was, but never heard his Christian name.

Limpy placed his hand on the Bible, and was sworn by the bailiff. "Do you solemnly swear to tell the truth, the whole truth, and nothing but the truth, so help you God?"

"Uh-huh," Limpy said.

"Say I do."

"You do."

"No, I do. You say I do,"

"I do."

Limpy glanced around, wide-eyed as a tourist getting his first glimpse of the Grand Canyon. He never before was called to testify at trial, for in his entire lackluster career as a peace officer it wasn't necessary that Limpy see the inside of a courtroom. He swiped a nervous hand across his face, nodded toward the jury box with an uneasy smile, and waved at the jurors before taking his seat in the witness stand.

Limpy looked at Will Starkey, who deposed him the week before, with an expression that said, "What am I doing here?"

"Now, Deputy Logan," Starkey said, "I'm Will Starkey. Do you recall our talk a while back?"

"Yes, I do."

"And do you recall what we talked about in our earlier conversation?"

"Well, yeah. We talked about John Willingham killing that woman."

"Objection!" Bates shouted. "It has not been established that the defendant was in any way responsible for the death of Josie Cramer."

"Sustained." Yokum instructed the court reporter, a dark-haired young woman, to "strike that."

"Deputy Logan," Starkey went on, "tell the Court in your own words what you recall about what happened that Sunday evening."

"Which year?"

Starkey's eyes sought wisdom in the peeling white plaster of the ceiling. "This year," he said, pleading to the gods for strength and endurance to help him. If this was his star witness, he could already feel his case slipping away. "Sunday August 20. Do you recall what took place that night?"

"Yeah, I do."

Starkey waited for Limpy to tell him.

Limpy stared at him with the blankest expression Starkey ever saw.

"Did anything unusual happen that night, deputy, that you recall?"

"Yeah, it did."

"Would you please explain to the Court exactly what was unusual about the night of August 20th?"

"I got a phone call from John."

"John—?"

"Huh?"

"John who, deputy?"

"Willin'ham. John Willin'ham. He called me."

"And what was unusual about that phone call from Mr. Willingham?"

"Never got one from him before."

Starkey checked to be sure the exit at the back of the chamber was open in case he had to make an abrupt departure. It could happen at any moment if this witness's testimony was the best he could do. "Is Mr. Willingham in the courtroom?"

"Yeah, he is," Limpy said.

"Would you be good enough to point out Mr. John Willingham for the jury?"

"He's setting right over there." Limpy pointed at John, seated next to Charlie Bates at the defense table. "He's the one in the checkered shirt."

"Tell the Court at what time on Sunday evening you received the call from Mr. John Williingham?"

"A little after seven o'clock, I'd judge."

"When you say a little after seven, does that mean two minutes, five minutes, ten minutes after seven?"

"Mebby ten after."

"So, you received the call from Mr. Willingham at about ten minutes past seven on Sunday evening. And Mr. Willingham told you what?"

"He told me that woman was dead."

"Did Mr. Willingham mention the woman's name?"

"Well, yeah, he did. He said it was Josie Cramer."

"Did you then go to the home of Josie Cramer?"

"I did."

"And when you arrived there, you found what?"

By this time Limpy was beginning to wonder which of the two of them—Starkey or himself—was loony, since they went through all that during the investigation the week before.

"John Willin'ham," Limpy said.

"You found John Willingham at Josie's home, and it was Mr. Willingham who called you at ten minutes past seven and told you Josie Cramer was dead?"

"Yes, sir, he did."

"Would you describe for the Court exactly what Mr. Willingham did after you arrived at the home of Josie Cramer?''

"He showed me the body."

"Whose body?"

Limpy gave him a shocked look that said, "Who do you think we're talking about here?"

The judge said, "Just answer the question, deputy."

"Whose body did Mr. Willingham show you?" Starkey said.

"Josie Cramer's."

"Thank you. And did you make an inspection of the body of Josie Cramer at that time?"

"I did."

"And what did you find?"

"She was dead."

Arthur Hicks, in the second row, gave his head an incredulous shake. This was the man on whom he depended to keep the peace in Blessing?

John stirred uncomfortably. He gave Bates a look that said he was ready for this to be over. Bates showed him a calming hand.

In the back of the room, Clara dabbed at her eyes with a tear-stained white handkerchief.

On the row in front of her sat Rufus Bonebrake,

dispatched by Simon Colby to observe the proceedings and report to him.

Next to Rufus was a young man named Dudley Coe. Dudley was wearing a heavy sheepskin coat he never removed in the court room. During Logan's testimony, Dudley nudged Rufus with a foolish grin. Rufus knew Dudley but didn't expect him to attend the trial. He looked at Coe as if he hadn't noticed he was there.

Louise Whitworth parked herself near the rail behind the defense table, so she could hear everything that went on. Louise didn't think what she knew about that Sunday night would contribute to the case, but was willing to testify in John's defense if called to do so.

Clovis Groop led the cheers of his faithful as they applauded the parts of the proceedings they agreed with.

Judge Yokum pounded his gavel for silence and got it.

"This court will tolerate no further disturbance," he said. "You may continue, counselor."

Starkey said to Logan, "After you examined the body of Josie Cramer, did you arrive at a conclusion as to what caused her death?"

"Yes sir, I did."

"Would you tell the Court what that conclusion was?"

"Her neck was broke."

"Objection!" Bates said. "This witness is not qualified to determine the cause of death."

"Sustained."

"You determined that her neck was broken," Starkey turned his back on the witness and faced the jury. "Were you then able to determine the cause of Miss Cramer's broken neck?"

"I figgered her and Mr. Willin'ham got into some kind of set-to, and he—"

"Objection! Your Honor, this testimony is totally without foundation."

To Starkey, Yokum said, "Counselor, at what point do you feel we might find our way back to relevancy?"

"Your Honor, this witness is not an expert," Bates protested. "His testimony is based solely on conjecture."

"You may continue," Yokum said to Starkey, "if you make it clear the witness's testimony is not based on established fact."

"With due respect, Your Honor," Bates said, "this witness's opinion is irrelevant, and may wrongfully influence the jury, which apparently is counsel's intent."

"Overruled. I want to hear what he has to say," Yokum said.

"Thank you, Your Honor," Starkey said. "In your opinion, Deputy Logan, was Mr. John Willingham the last person to see Josie Cramer alive?"

"Yes, sir, he was."

"And did that lead you to believe John Willingham choked her until her neck was broken, leading to the death of Josie Cramer?"

Limpy took a long look at John. "Yes, sir," he gulped.

"Satisfied that Mr. John Willingham was the last person to see Josie Cramer alive, and he was the one who choked her until her neck was broken, which you believe led to her death—Deputy Logan, did you then take Mr. Willingham into custody for the murder of Josie Cramer?"

"Yes, sir, I did."

Starkey flipped through his notes on the blue-lined yellow pages. "I have no further questions at this time, Your Honor," he said. "We may want to re-direct at a later time."

"Mr. Bates?" Yokum said.

Charlie checked his notes, and whispered something to John. John shook his head as though he didn't agree with his lawyer's whispered consultation.

Even so, Bates said, "We have no questions at this time, Your Honor."

Judge Yokum gave Bates a startled look, puzzled that he was not going to cross examine the witness. He then banged his gavel.

"Because of the time, and the pressure of the Court's docket," Herman P. said, "this court is adjourned until nine o'clock next Wednesday. Does counsel agree?"

Bates shook his head no, but reluctantly joined Starkey who agreed to the delay.

"All rise." The gallery got to its collective feet and waited for Judge Yokum to disappear through the door of his chamber behind the bench.

Even the judge, in all his wisdom, couldn't have foreseen what Wednesday morning brought to his court room.

DAVID A. ESTES

CHAPTER 15

Herman's dilemma

By Saturday noon, Judge Yokum was fidgeting about the house.

He applied Miracle Gro to his prize tomatoes, and pinched the dead blossoms off the red geraniums in the flower beds surrounding the house.

He hated those big ugly hollyhocks Pauline thought she needed to plant because her sister gave her the seeds. Hollyhocks in full bloom he approved, but once the blooms were gone, they looked like wilted nine-foot noodles.

That morning Herman herded his sixteen-horse John Deere riding mower over the acre of lush green grass envious neighbors accused him of manicuring with tweezers.

He cherished the time he spent mowing. The drone of the motor drowned out the cacophony of legalese that saturated his brain in court all week.

The joy of playing farmer this day, however, was diminished by the dilemma of the John Willingham trial. Herman didn't like what he heard from the prosecution's witness.

The blank expression on Willingham's face remained static throughout the proceedings, and Yokum heard nothing from the defense table, except when Bates objected to something Starkey said.

The judge was well aware of the danger of becoming emotionally involved in a court case. His responsibility was to observe, Listen, and pass judgment according to the law after all evidence was presented. Most cases had a "smell" to them by which he could detect some semblance of guilt or innocence, but this one didn't smell right. Herman puzzled over Willingham's frowning reaction to Bates' not guilty plea, and by Charlie's no questions for the witness on Friday.

Herman wouldn't hazard a guess as to how long the trial would last. Some trials ran for months, depending on the severity of the crime, and how long it took the lawyers to present evidence. And, sad to say, he knew of cases in which "equal justice for all" depended on the social or financial status of the person occupying the defendant's seat.

In Herman's court, however, every defendant was viewed with the same consideration as the last one, and many cases were wrapped up in a handful of sessions. He hoped this one wouldn't drag out into a protracted series of episodes between defense and prosecution because his wife Pauline pestered him to take her to see her aging mother in St. Louis four hundred miles away. He didn't want to go, but he'd rather go and get it over with than endure another six months of Pauline's nagging about it.

Length of the Willingham trial depended on how many witnesses Starkey rounded up, and how many times Bates objected.

Starkey, as Arthur Hicks predicted, sought a delay until after he returned from his African safari, but Yokum nixed that.

Disposition of the Willingham case took precedence over the prosecutor's thrill of hunting down some irate jungle beast that wasn't ready to die.

So far, Starkey hadn't made much of a case. That so-called deputy, in the mind of the judge, was not a credible witness, and damaged Starkey's case more than it helped.

With a practiced eye, Judge Yokum observed the jury's reaction to testimony. Facial expressions, eye movement, and body language often told him what they were thinking, indicating how the trial was going, for the prosecution or the defense. The Willingham jury, however, gave him little to go on. They were as stolid as a herd of cattle—all facing the same direction, seeing and hearing the same testimony, but displaying no emotion that told him whether they believed Willingham committed the crime Starkey was trying to nail him for.

Maybe the jury was waiting for Starkey to shut up so they could hear what Bates had to say, since the defense lawyer said nothing constructive.

Either way, the judge heard nothing on which to form an opinion.

Pauline learned from thirty-six years of living under the same roof with the judge that Herman P. was in a rare stew about something all weekend.

Pauline was pretty sure it had to do with the Willingham trial, but she hesitated to ask. The judge didn't tolerate inquisition unless he was the one asking the questions. She knew better than to invade his private mulling while he was sitting in judgment.

Herman clung to his practice of not discussing a case with her until after the verdict. About this one, however, he appeared abnormally pensive. Hardly did he speak to her since he got home from court on Friday. During dinner last night, he was strangely quiet, totally out of character for the usually affable judge, especially with the kids there, celebrating grandson Sean's eleventh birthday.

"What's the matter with Dad?" Sean's mother Lettie asked Pauline while they were clearing away after dinner.

Pauline cast her a wide-eyed your-guess-is-as-good-as-mine look, and didn't elaborate because she'd have to explain something she knew nothing about, and wouldn't know until after the Willingham trial.

At the Sunday morning church service, Herman's strong tenor was absent from the choir's rendering of hymns he usually sang with gusto. Through "praise God from whom all blessings flow" he stood beside her in the congregation silent as Mount Rushmore.

On their way out after the service, he shook Reverend Doyle's hand as limply as if he didn't know to whose arm it was attached.

Responding to the reverend's curious nod and, "What's bothering the judge?" Pauline gave him a noncommittal shrug with an I-wish-I-knew shake of her head.

Monday morning the judge didn't move out of the house. Instead, he closeted himself in his study. He uttered not a word of explanation for why he didn't head for the office, a ritual since he passed the bar nearly forty years before. Pauline had watched him crawl out of bed when he could hardly breathe from a head cold that would have prostrated most of his peers for days, but somehow Herman dragged himself to the office.

By mid-afternoon she'd had it up to her ear bobs with his reticence. The faraway look in his eyes told her his mind was someplace else.

"Why don't you go fishing?" Pauline said.

"What?"

"Fishing, judge." She called him judge when she could no longer stand the sight of him. "Why don't you go fishing?"

He cringed. From the tone of her voice, Herman knew he struck the nerve that made Pauline turn mean.

"Call Sean and take him with you," she said. "He'll be ready by the time you get there. Go wet a hook and get out from under my feet."

Sean was waiting in the driveway with his fishing rod and tackle box when his granddad braked his spotless blue VW Beetle to a stop.

Hardly had they reached their favorite spot where the blue gill ran, and got their lines in the water, before Sean posed a disturbing query.

"Mom said for me to find out why you've been such a pain in the ass lately," Sean said.

Herman laid upon his grandson a look of total shock.

"Your mother said that?"

"Yeah. She's worried about you, granddad."

Herman ruffled Sean's blond head with an affectionate palm.

"Maybe after Wednesday I can let her know," he said.

CHAPTER 16

Tuesday before Wednesday court

Starkey slid into the booth where Bates was sipping at a bottle of Bud at the Modern Vets Bar.

Twelve years ago they sat next to each other at a Bar Association dinner, learned they grew up in neighboring communities, traded stories, and became friends. They golfed on weekends, their wives belonged to the Methodist church circle and played bridge together, and their kids attended the same public school.

In the court room, Will and Charlie were fierce competitors, but privately, each held the other in high regard. Like two wrestlers walking away arm-in-arm after the match, no matter who won.

A leggy blond waitress in a short leather skirt appeared and asked Starkey what she could bring him to drink. He ordered a Bloody Mary. Bates asked for another beer.

"It looks like your man is going down," Starkey said as the waitress turned away.

"Is that so?"

"He has no alibi."

"Except that he was nowhere near the crime scene when the murder was committed."

"So he says."

"So he says. And we have witnesses," Bates said, "who will testify to that."

"Who are they?"

"The man who gave Willingham a lift into town, for beginners."

"Martin?"

"Dude Martin."

"You can't count on his testimony," the prosecutor challenged. "He's half hostile. When I talked to him he wasn't even sure what time he picked Willingham up."

"He wasn't under oath then."

"His memory won't get any better once he's sworn."

The waitress brought their drinks and turned away. "That deputy of yours," Charlie said, sipping at his beer, "is about as credible as going over Niagara Falls in a hula hoop."

In addition to Martin, Bates would call Lena Bradley and Ernie Phipps to verify John's whereabouts at the time Logan said Josie was killed.

Apparently Starkey thought his case strong enough without even deposing Lena and Ernie, totally unlike the usually meticulous prosecutor.

Safaris didn't happen every day, Charlie

conceded, but Will needed to get his head out of Africa and into the court room.

Lena told Bates that John hadn't drunk anything at the Welcome Back, counter to John's description of what happened between himself and Josie. So deepened the mystery of why John appeared anxious to convict himself of murder.

"You're a good friend, Charlie, and I hate to see this happen to you," Starkey said, "but your boy is going down."

Bates took another sip at his beer. Starkey didn't know anything he didn't know. Will's favorite device in the court room was intimidation.

That deputy, as Charlie characterized Logan, was a foolish ass who obviously wished he were someplace else during Starkey's cross examination.

Bates knew Logan was in way over his head, and wouldn't recognize a homicide if somebody bought him a ticket to it.

Starkey got up to leave. "See you in court," he said.

"I'll be there." With a grin, he added, "You bring the beer."

Four o'clock in the morning

Clara flipped on the light and glanced at the clock on the bedside table. Four-thirty-four Wednesday morning. It was well past midnight when she finally got to bed, and she hardly slept.

Until she heard the clock strike twelve, she rummaged around, doing things that didn't need doing. She looked for some way to erase the distressing image of her son, slumped like a stump in that court room chair. He'd be there again in a few hours, acting like he didn't care one way or the other how things turned out. She'd be there, agonizing over the maddening silence of Charlie Bates who did nothing in John's defense.

Through sleepless nights, Clara turned Logan's testimony over and over in her mind. She knew in her heart John did not kill that woman, but she was helpless to do anything about it.

And yes, she was angry enough to shove Josie against the chiffarobe, but not hard enough to kill her. Had she? Still, not knowing muddled her mind and kept her awake, tossing and turning all night from one position to another until she might have worn holes in the bed sheets.

Her tears were all shed, and her prayers all said. Where could she turn for answers? She threw off the covers, pulled on a robe, and was on her way to the kitchen to put the coffee pot on when the jangle of the phone gave her a start. Why would anyone be calling at this hour? Calls before daylight always brought bad news.

She grabbed the phone, and said, "Hello."

"He never done it," she heard a man's high-pitched voice say.

Clara's hand was shaky as a dried oak leaf. "What? Who is this?" she said.

"He never killed the whore," the man said.

The line went dead. In a daze, Clara hung up. She didn't know what it meant. She said a silent prayer that the voice referred to John, but she wasn't sure she had heard right.

Stumbling toward the kitchen, she burst into

tears. She had to do something—put the coffee pot on! Put away the clean dishes she struggled to get done last night, though her mind was miles away from dirty dishes. Scrub the kitchen floor. Do anything to occupy her mind. She hoped the man on the phone, whoever he was, knew what he was talking about.

Since John was arrested, Clara wrestled with the Pontiac and made her way to the jail to visit him almost every day until it became too heavy an emotional burden. There was not much they could talk about. Work on the farm was at a standstill.

John was adamant about "getting this thing over with." She struggled to keep from breaking down where everybody could see, but burst into tears on the way home.

At the trial, she sat on the back row, silently sniffling, watching helplessly as the proceedings unfolded. Wishing Charlie Bates would do something!

When it was time for her to go again that morning, she backed the Pontiac out and headed for the courthouse. Recent experience bolstered her confidence behind the wheel, and she even learned to park as long as there were no other cars within crashing distance. She followed the crowd, and took her seat on the back row of the court room. She searched the faces around her for one that matched the voice she heard on the phone. "He never done it."

If Simon Colby's arthritis hadn't backed up on him, he'd have parked his bulk on the front row of the gallery at every session of the trial. He'd be there to show his respect for John Willingham. Rufus was supposed to keep him posted, but the errant preacher's accounts of the proceedings were questionable.

Ernie invited Simon to ride to the court house with him, but Simon declined, fat and "stove up" as he was. He sent word to Clara and John of his concern about the outcome of the trial and would like to be there, but there was no one he could depend on to keep the store open while he was gone.

Ernie took another day off from the packing plant to attend the trial on Wednesday. He thought Bates might call him as a witness because he talked to John at the Welcome Back before the murder.

He stopped by the Sak 'n Pak for a pack of Luckies on his way to the court house.

Simon asked Ernie how it was going.

"John said he done it, you know," Ernie said.

"No, I didn't know John said he done it."

"Well, he ain't said he didn't do it."

"That's not the same as saying he done it."

"Anyhow that's what they're trying to stick him with."

"You think he done it, Ernie?"

"I don't know what to think, Si. Dude Martin said on the TV news John's got a hellish temper at times. I don't know about that, but I wouldn't think they'd nail him to the cross just for killing a whore."

Josie made occasional visits to the Sak 'n Pak and paid cash for everything she left with. In spite of her past, and the gossip from the flapping gums had maligned her unmercifully, Simon disregarded her past, letting it stay the past. He pegged Josie as a decent lady who did nothing wrong since she came to town.

Josie found out when Simon's birthday was, and brought him his favorite German chocolate cake with candles on it.

"Whores are people too," he said to Ernie. "We don't know everything. Besides that, she give up whoring before she come to town."

"I guess you could call 'em that," Ernie said.

"Call who what?"

"Whores people."

Simon sliced off a chunk of baked ham from the meat case and stuffed it in his mouth.

"John and Josie was pretty close," he said. "But I reckon it don't take much sometimes for a feller to go off the deep end."

"Yeah, when I was rodeoing," Ernie said, "I seen 'em snap like that over something that didn't amount to nothing." Ernie demonstrated with a snap of his fingers.

"John's got a good lawyer though," Si said.

"Yeah, Charlie's good. So far, he ain't done much for John though."

"When do you reckon it'll be over?"

"No way to tell," Ernie said. "Bates is supposed to do his thing today. John acts like he don't give a hoot in hell one way or the other."

"That ain't like John."

"I'm going again today. Me and Rufus. I keep thinking Bates might call on me to say something."

"You want to?"

"No. But if it'd help John, I would. Somebody needs to be helping him. It don't look like he cares about helping himself. Most of the time he just sits there stiff as a poker."

"You think he done it, Ernie?"

Ernie shook his head. "I hope to hell he didn't."

CHAPTER 17

All rise.

The jury showed Herman P. nothing that told him which way the trial was going, and Willingham's reaction to testimony told him less. Herman didn't know John Willingham, and never saw him before the arraignment when John took a seat beside Charlie Bates.

Still, the judge was puzzled. John's interest in the court process was evinced by his look of protest when Bates objected at certain points of Logan's testimony. In the mind of Judge Yokum, John's reaction cast a shadow of doubt over the proceedings. So far, Bates did nothing on John's behalf aside from scribbling notes on his pad. Herman was eager to hear Bates break his silence with whatever he had to present in John's defense.

He wondered whether either Bates or Starkey would call Willingham to the stand. Starkey would gain little by crossing John, except as a last ditch effort to salvage his case. Bates needed to make some kind of positive move on the part of his client.

The judge settled behind the bench and pounded his gavel. "Mr. Bates?"

Charlie checked his notes. "Thank you, Your Honor. Defense calls Deputy Logan."

Once again, Limpy was escorted into the courtroom. He was already sworn, so he didn't have to stumble through it again.

Charlie ambled over to the witness box where Limpy awaited his arrival.

"Reckon what he wants?" was the first thing that popped into the mind of the uneasy deputy.

Bates took his time getting there, letting Limpy stew.

"Now, Deputy Logan," Charlie said upon his arrival. "But, I believe in the city of Blessing you're known as the sheriff. Is that correct, sir?"

"That's what some folks call me, yes, sir."

"And how long have the folks of Blessing been calling you the sheriff?"

"Ever since the county started paying me to be a deputy."

"And how long ago was that, sir?"

"I believe it was seven years ago. Arthur Hicks promised me a raise if—"

"You were not elected to the position of deputy? By that I mean, you didn't have to run for the office, like Sheriff Hicks there, or my colleague, Mr. Starkey?"

"No."

"Actually, sir, would it be fair to say that

Sheriff Hicks appointed you to the position of deputy sheriff for the city of Blessing because nobody else wanted the job?"

"Objection!" Starkey shouted. "Intimidating the witness."

"Sustained. Strike that," the judge said, and the bespectacled court reporter did as she was told.

"If the Court please," Bates said, "our purpose is to establish the credibility of this witness."

"The witness has been sworn and examined," Starkey said.

"I will allow it, Mr. Bates," Yokum said, "as long as you are pursuing a valid point."

"Thank you, sir. Now, Deputy Logan," Charlie said to the witness, "does the job of deputy sheriff in Blessing require all your time? Is it a full-time job?"

"No, sir, I—"

"In what activities do you engage besides serving as deputy sheriff?"

"Well, I fish some."

"Bass fishing, isn't it?"

"Yes, sir. Bass fishing. And I coon hunt sometimes too when—"

"Is it not true, sir, that when you're not bass fishing or coon hunting, or playing sheriff in the city of Blessing, that you spend an inordinate amount of time in bed?"

"Your Honor, please!" Starkey pleaded. "This line of questioning is totally irrelevant."

"Hold on, counselor," Yokum said to Starkey. To Bates, he said, "are we approaching a point here, counselor?"

"Yes, Your Honor. Please bear with me for another minute."

"You may proceed," the judge said, "as long as you are pursuing a relevant point."

"Thank you, Your Honor." Back to Limpy, Charlie said, "Now, Mr. Logan, you testified that Mr. John Willingham called you on Sunday evening August 20th, about ten minutes after seven."

"Yes, sir, he did."

"And where were you at that time, sir, at seven o'clock on a Sunday evening?"

"Well, where I was, was—"

"He was in bed asleep," Louise called from the audience. "I'm Louise Whitworth. I woke him up to tell him about it."

A twitter made its way around the courtroom. Some of the jurors hid amused smiles behind their hands, and the Groop group scowled their displeasure.

Judge Yokum pounded his gavel.

"Any further disturbance and this courtroom will be cleared." He settled back into his chair, wondering whether what he heard from Bates was as strong as his cross examination was going to get. If so, he needed to find something better to talk about. To Charlie, he said, "You may proceed, Mr. Bates, but we would appreciate it if you would hasten to arrive at wherever it is you're taking us."

"Thank you, Your Honor. Now, Mr. Logan, you testified that you went to the home of Josie Cramer, viewed the body, and—"

"She was dead."

"—pronounced her dead. And Mr. John

Willingham, whom you earlier pointed out to the jury, was at the home of the deceased when you arrived. Is that correct?"

"Yeah, he was."

"After examining the body you determined that Miss Cramer's neck was broken. And in your opinion, sir, her broken neck caused her death."

"That's what I figgered."

"According to the record, you also testified, after questioning him, in your opinion, John Willingham was the last person to see Miss Cramer alive. Is that a true statement, sir?"

"I reckon."

"Is that a yes?"

"Yes, sir."

"Thank you. And because you believed he was the last person to see her alive, you suspected Mr. Willingham of the death of Josie Cramer. Have I stated that correctly?"

"Yes, sir, you have."

"Now, having determined in your mind that John Willingham was the one who caused the death of Josie Cramer, you told the Court you arrested him for that crime."

"I did."

"And what did you do after you arrested him?"

The gallery waited while Limpy stewed.

"I turned him loose," said the deputy.

"You turned him loose?" Bates said, addressing the jury. "You arrested John Willingham for the murder of Josie Cramer, and you turned him loose?"

"Yeah, I did."

The gallery reacted with a buzz, exchanging confused looks from furrowed brows, whispering among themselves, casting dubious glances at the jury box.

If the arresting officer released the primary suspect, the jurors counseled each other with questioning expressions, how could Deputy Logan testify that John Willingham was guilty of the crime? Equally confusing was the question: If Willingham did not commit the murder, why did he turn himself in, and why was he now on trial for the murder?

Bates studied the muddled expressions on the faces of the jury, which consisted of four women and eight men. He gave them a moment to absorb the significance of the deputy's statement.

To the gallery, Charlie said, "Is it not true, Deputy Logan, after you turned him loose, you gave Mr. Willingham a ride home?"

"Well, yeah, he was afoot, and—"

Will Starkey glared at the witness, struck by the reality that his examination stopped one question short of the one whose answer might have averted his looking like a fool.

Arthur Hicks palmed his chin, shook his head in disbelief, and stared at his boots.

"Mr. Logan," Bates said, "your testimony is that you arrested John Willingham for the murder of Josie Cramer. And you —"

"I let him go."

"—let him go. Now, would you be good enough to explain to the Court why you released the man you arrested for the murder of Josie Cramer?"

"I didn't have nothin' on him."

Starkey paled, and slid deeper into his chair.

Judge Yokum leaned forward to be sure he heard right.

To Limpy, the judge said, "Would you say that again, please?"

"I never had nothin' solid on him," Limpy said.

The judge sank back into his chair with a questioning look at Will Starkey.

"You let him go, deputy," Bates said loud and clear, to be sure the jury didn't mistake his words, "because you had nothing on him.

"Does that mean, sir, that you found no evidence, though in your opinion he was the last person to see her alive, that in any way implicates Mr. John Willingham in the death of Josie Cramer?"

"Yes, sir. That's what it means."

"And in your opinion, Deputy Logan, since you found no reason to hold Mr. John Willingham for the murder of Miss Cramer, do you now believe he did not commit the crime for which he is on trial?"

"Well, I—"

"Your witness."

Starkey was in no hurry, chafing still from the unforgivable blunder a first year law student wouldn't commit. The question he didn't asked Logan was, "Did you lock John Willingham in jail for the murder of Josie Cramer?"

Logan threw him a curve, and Starkey swung too soon. He'd gain nothing by further questioning the witless deputy who released the only suspect in the case because he "didn't have nothin' solid on him."

Starkey checked his notes, searching for something that would tell him what to do next. The gallery waited. From the midst of the gallery, the silence was shattered by a high-pitched voice.

CHAPTER 18

"He never done it."

Clara's heart leaped, recognizing unmistakably the voice she heard on the phone at four-thirty-four that morning! Whose voice was it?

The jury stirred uneasily. The spectators murmured among themselves, bewildered by what was taking place. They, like Clara, wondered to whom the voice belonged, and why they heard it now.

Starkey jerked his head about. Bates craned his neck to see where the disruptive outburst came from.

Judge Yokum was so taken aback he didn't even pound his gavel.

All heads turned, eyes settling on the grinning, unshaven twenty-four-year-old man in the sheepskin coat, and the St. Louis Cardinals baseball cap, sitting next to Rufus Bonebrake.

Rufus knew Dudley Coe. They attended ball games together. Rufus even bought him hot dogs and beer. Even so, with Dudley's outburst, Rufus looked at him like he never saw him before. He couldn't believe Coe had the grit to interrupt the courtroom proceedings.

A snicker swept the room when the audience realized the young man was a simple handy-man around town who did odd jobs for many of them.

Hamp Hargrove was sitting alone on the row half way back. His face turned ashen.

"He never done it," Coe said again. His broad grin reflected pleasure at being so recognized. "But I know who did," Coe said.

John's head jerked around like the swivel on a chair. Who the hell—

The bench glared in shocked silence. Neither the prosecution nor the defense found its voice in protest of the unheard of interruption.

The gallery stirred in disbelief. Some emitted nervous chuckles.

"You want me to come down there?" Dudley said, unabashed.

Clara could hardly breathe. A hand went to her trembling lips. If they allowed him to testify, what would he say? He said he knew who killed Josie. The sisters said they saw nobody go into, nor out of Josie's house.

But this man must have seen somebody. What if he saw John there? Or, if not John— Whose name might he blurt out?

Starkey finally requested the man be removed from the court room.

"If he has something to contribute to this case, Your Honor," Bates countered, "with due respect, this man deserves to be heard."

Starkey repeated his protest.

Judge Yokum said, "Gentlemen, approach the bench."

John, alone at the defense table, watched Bates and Starkey huddle with the judge. He saw their heads alternately nod and shake. He tried to interpret Starkey's arm-waving at Charlie Bates. John wasn't sure he wanted to hear what the intruder had to say. Was Coe at Josie's that night? What was he doing there? Did he see who else was there, and did he really know who killed Josie Cramer? Or was the handyman, for whatever reason, only taking advantage of an opportunity to draw attention to himself?

Yokum won the round at the bench, and sent Bates and Starkey back to their tables. John questioned the significance of the development to which the judge referred as "highly irregular," but allowed it to continue. Bates showed John a calming palm. John didn't want to hear the name he was afraid Coe might blurt out.

Charlie dared not speculate on the outcome of Coe's testimony. But if the man knew anything that might support John's case—"he never done it"—he wanted to hear it.

Starkey wasn't pleased with the disruptive occurrence, but Coe was called and sworn.

"You bet," Coe said with a broad grin, his hand on the King James Version.

The bailiff instructed Dudley to remove his

baseball cap. Dudley did, and a mop of disheveled black hair tumbled down over his forehead. He began talking like a man who never before was asked what he thought.

"I never had no schooling much," Coe began. "My daddy scratched a living out of the hills, and when I got big enough, I helped him scratch. Me and my five brothers.

"Never had no sisters. My mama done all the woman work. Scrubbing, cooking, sewing, taking care of us. Praying for us when somebody got down."

Starkey listened in disbelief. It appeared that Dudley's tale, whatever it was, was likely to take more time than it deserved.

Will returned to his seat at the table, wondering why in hell Herman Yokum allowed this man to relate his life story, except that Coe asked for time "to tell why?"

Bates listened with rapt attention, along with the jury.

Judge Yokum leaned forward and cupped a hand to his right ear.

John's breath came hard and fast, not knowing what to expect from Dudley's rambling testimony, afraid of what it might reveal.

"When I was fourteen," Dudley went on, "Mama got to where she couldn't do it no more, and she died. I watched her suffering and paining and praying that God would take her, and one day he did. With her dying breath she told me I was the best kid she had. I prayed I wouldn't never have to go through what she did, and I never did. But my boy did.

"When I was nineteen I brung Sara Jo home and told papa her and me was married. The next year, Sara Jo went into the back room. After a while she come out carrying a squalling little baby boy. Papa was prouder than a heifer with a newborn calf. We named the boy Wesley 'cause that was papa's name. Not long after that, papa died of the fever.

"Little Wesley was four year old when he come down with it. The doctor told me and Sara Jo if he didn't have proper caring for right away he was gonna die. Mama was gone, and nobody else knew how to lick the fever.

"Sara Jo was gonna leave me and take little Wesley with her lest I done something for him. They wasn't no money, and no groceries on the place, so— Well, I just about hit the bottom of the well.

"I heard about Miz Cramer being a whore and all, like everybody else did,I'd say. I heard folks talking about how whores made a lot of money, and I figured maybe she had some, and I'd get it for little Wesley.

"So, what I done was, I snuck around her house, looking for some way I could get in and out again without nobody knowing it. I got to this window where the shade was up enough for me to peek in under it, and there she was, all nekkid and everything. That's when I heard the doorbell ring. I seen her put on that robe, and she went to see who was at the door, I guess. I about got scared outa what I come to do.

"Then I heard these voices hollering at each

other. Miz Cramer, she come running back into the bedroom. This older lady was chasing her, calling her names, and grabbing at her, and flung her up against the chiffarobe. Miz Cramer, she never got up, like she was dead."

John steeled himself against what he feared was coming next.

Clara hardly blinked. She sat stone still and covered her face up to her eyes with the tear-stained handkerchief. Coe said John "never done it." Did that mean he saw her kill Josie?

"The older lady run out then," Dudley went on, "and I heard the front door slam.

"I took a little time to think on what I oughta do. Finally it come to me that if Miz Cramer was dead, I could go in her house, find where she kept the money, and get out without nobody knowing.

"So, what I done was, I eased into the front door. I wondered where to start looking. Then it come to me most people hid money in their bedroom. So, I snuck into the bedroom, and there she was, sprawled out on the floor, nekkider'n a jaybird.

"I guess I must've forgot what I come for, and I done it to 'er. I never done it to a dead woman before, but I done it to her. Well, see, I thought she was dead, but by the time I got done doin' 'er, she commenced to wriggle and squirm. Her eyes popped open, and she started yelling and screaming and hitting me with her fists and I couldn't make her stop.

"I grabbed her by the throat and she still didn't shut up, so I choked her a little to get her to stop, but she never did. I squeezed a little harder, and I guess that's when it happened. She quit screaming, and she didn't move no more. And that's how I done it."

Except for a smattering of coughs and sniffles and clearing of throats, silence reigned. The astonished gallery tried to figure out how this witless young handy man could commit such a deed.

Starkey scratched his nose while he thought about what to do next. He got up from the table and approached the witness. "What about the boy?" he asked Dudley.

"Little Wesley, he died."

"And Sara Jo?"

"Gone. She's gone too."

"Dead?"

"Just gone."

The prosecutor, recognized by his peers as an in-control practitioner of the law devoid of emotion, said, "Are you sorry for what you did?"

"Well, see, I never done it to a dead wom—"

Starkey backhanded Dudley across the mouth, a stinging blow that knocked him out of his chair and against the witness box. The bug-eyed Dudley, bleeding from the mouth, threw up his arms to protect himself from further blows. The fuming Starkey wheeled around, half way to the door at the back of the courtroom on his way out.

The crowd gasped in disbelief.

Judge Yokum pounded his gavel and shouted something legal like "in contempt."

Will strode toward the exit past the court

officer without a backward glance.

"Yeah, right, Your Honor," Starkey muttered to nobody, bursting out the door of the courtroom. "Guilty as charged."

"I never done it to a dead woman before."

Starkey was angry and disgusted. He was angry and disgusted at other times for other reasons, but never did he give in to the urge to explode at a witness's testimony. No remorse. No shame. It was like Coe was proud of violating the body of a dead woman. As ifhe'd do it again given the chance.

"Dumb ass!" Starkey seethed on his way out.

The click of his departing footsteps bounced off the courthouse walls. Across his mind flashed a quote from Oscar Wilde: The best way to deal with temptation is to yield to it.

Starkey did.

Dudley's chilling account of "how I done it" left no doubt in the minds of the judge, the jury, and the stunned spectators of how Josie Cramer died.

In the opinion of Judge Yokum, however, Dudley's confession was not sufficient to convict him of the crime. Though his doubts of John Willingham's guilt were confirmed by the young man's testimony, Herman questioned whether Dudley was mentally capable of understanding the gravity of the crime he confessed. He ordered Dudley held for mental examination until it could be determined whether he was capable of standing trial, or being committed to the psychiatric ward.

Herman's concern, during the trial, was John's showing no interest in being absolved of the crime. It hung around like a pesky mosquito. The record showed only that John Willingham turned himself in, stood trial, and was found innocent of the murder of Josie Cramer.

The judge felt pity for Dudley Coe.

Still, Herman couldn't suppress the hint of a smile after Dudley was ushered from the chamber by a court officer, pleased that Will Starkey didn't round up enough horses to nail Willingham to the cross for a crime he didn't commit.

One day down the road, if examination should find Dudley capable of standing trial, a brilliant young barrister would be assigned by the Court the responsibility of proving him guilty of murder. And some brilliant old barrister, maybe Charlie Bates, likely would present evidence proving Dudley was incapable of murder, possibly committing him for the rest of his life to an institution.

But that day would never come.

Three hours after Arthur Hicks locked Dudley in his jail, the body of the young, witless handyman was found with a broken neck, stuffed in the mess hall garbage can.

Questioned inmates feigned shock and dismay, protesting that they saw nothing and heard nothing, and, therefore, could provide no clue as to who was guilty of such a dastardly deed.

Bye-bye, Dudley

Coe's funeral wasn't a major event, even in Blessing, Oklahoma.

John Willingham saw Dudley around town once in a while, but recalled no words passing between them. Relieved as he was that Coe didn't mention his mother's name on the witness stand, Coe's description of how he "done it" to Josie sent bolts of anger surging through John's body. Even so, he came to Seth Gibbs's funeral parlor to pay last respects to the man whose confession might have saved his life.

John spotted Hampton Hargrove seated on the third row of Seth Gibbs's funeral chapel and wondered why he was there. He doubted Hamp knew Dudley any better than he did. But there Hamp was, sitting alone on the back pew of the chapel.

Simon Colby attended the funeral out of respect for the grinning, unassuming young man who delivered groceries for him, swept out the store, and often spent the night on the cot in Simon's back room.

Seated on the front pew where he could hear what was taking place, Simon shed no tears for Dudley. He was sorry Dudley lost his wife and son. At times he felt pity for the young man. But Simon did not weep for him. He shed no tears even when he learned his son Isaac was killed, but dry eyes were no measure of his sorrow. Only once was Simon reduced to tears, the day Thelma died. There were still private times when he paid tearful tribute to the memory of the wife he dearly loved.

But no tears did Simon shed for Dudley Coe.

Limpy Logan didn't want to miss a good day for bass fishing, so he made himself scarce by not showing up at Dudley's funeral.

Benny Pelham attended to cover the event for the Blessing Blessing.

Skelly Wilks sat as far away as he could get from the closed casket at the front of the chapel. He was afraid if he sat too close to the front, somebody might ask him to do something.

Parked on the front pew next to Simon were Ernie Phipps and Rufus Bonebrake. Their eyes were fixed on the wooden casket, half expecting Dudley to rise up at any moment and plop down on the seat beside them. They liked Dudley. They stood up for him at times against the taunts of insensitive bullies.

Clovis Groop sought, and received, the approval of Seth Gibbs to preside at Dudley's funeral. Groop's reasoning was he "was involved in the case" from the beginning. Why Groop hadn't done the same for Josie a few weeks earlier nobody knew. He grievously maligned her in the beginning, yet championed her cause after she was dead.

Josie's funeral went unnoticed, except for a brief account in Benny Pelham's weekly Blessing, as if the stigma of her past followed her to the grave, even though many lamented her departure.

Simon was one of a few who attended Josie's funeral.

John, awaiting trial in Arthur Hicks's jail, wasn't permitted to attend.

Groop's knowledge of Coe as a person was practically nil, and needed little time to share what he knew about him during the ceremony. Groop read the twenty-third Psalm from the King James Version, and recited a couple of short prayers, after which he sat by with a sad look on his face. Aging, blue-haired Goldie Oliver, in her quavering contralto, sang "Amazing Grace" and "How Great

Thou Art." Goldie collected her three dollars Seth paid her for singing at funerals of people she didn't know, and went home.

After Groop invoked the Lord to "wrap your love around this weary traveler," he called it good.

The casket remained closed as the mourners filed out. Hargrove was the last to leave.

On his way out, John saw Hamp move to the casket, and place his hand on it. John thought it strange, but strange people did strange things.

"Hamp?" Seth said quietly after everyone else was gone. He needed to get that casket in the ground.

"I know, Seth," Hargrove said. "I just wanted a minute."

"You knew Dudley, did you?"

With wistful eyes the big man peered at the undertaker. "He was my son," Hamp said.

Seth was shocked. He didn't know much about Hargrove's private life, but he never guessed he had a son, or even that he was ever married. "He was your son?" Seth said.

"Years ago, his mama and me—we—" Hamp cocked his head to one side.

Seth nodded as if he understood.

"He didn't know," Hargrove said. "Now he never will."

The giant with no left arm, and a menacing whisper for a voice—the enforcer—wept.

CHAPTER 19

Reunion

Clara and John found little to talk about when he got home from the funeral.

She sat frozen to her courtroom seat, eyes unblinking, when Dudley confessed to killing Josie. She shed body-wrenching tears when she was told he was found dead. She didn't attend the ceremony, but was assured that Seth buried Dudley in the Baptist Church cemetery, where he buried everybody else. It was over and done with. She tried to put it all out of her mind, and talking about it wouldn't be pleasant.

John's greatest relief was finding out Clara had nothing to do with Josie's death. He was glad it was over; glad Bates didn't call him to testify because he'd have to lie on the stand, perjuring himself. Or he'd have to tell the truth, condemning his mother whose innocence was proved by Dudley's tale. To himself, John confessed a sense of shame for silently pointing the finger of guilt at his mother. In time he would tell her.

He cranked up the Allis, hitched on the hay rack, and went to the house for a jug of fresh water to take with him to the field. He filled the jug from the kitchen pump and was on his way out the kitchen door when he heard Clara call to him.

"Yes, Mama?"

"I'm sorry, son," she said.

Talk had to come sometime. John guessed this was it. He responded with a silent nod.

"I never knew Josie," Clara said. "I was wrong about her." Clara's cheeks were wet with tears. Again she said, "I'm sorry."

"I know, Mama."

"I didn't go there to hurt her. I believed what she was doing to you was wrong."

"You did what you thought needed to be done."

"These past weeks," Clara said, "I've had time to do some thinking." She wiped her eyes on her apron. "I was worried sick all the time you were stuck in that jail. Then, seeing you sitting there, watching you in that courtroom, wanting to reach out to you, I wished I could comfort you. I knew you couldn't do that to her, or anybody else. I was afraid of what they might do to you.

"You turned yourself in because you thought I killed Josie. I knew that, but I couldn't bring myself to let you know. I didn't know how to tell you. And there I was, letting you do it, not turning a hand to do anything about it."

"There was nothing you could do, Mama."

"I've done some things I wish I hadn't, and I'd take them all back if I could," she cried. Like what I did to your father. We loved each other, but we never seemed able to get along well together. It wasn't all his fault. Much of the time I was not fair to him. I know now he left because of me, and I'll live with that for the rest of my life.

"I haven't been fair with you either, John, keeping you here on this farm when you wanted to be someplace else. I want you to know, if that's what you think is best, we'll sell the farm and move away from here."

"We need to talk about that."

"There is something else you need to know," she sniffled. "I'm sorry I treated Holly so badly."

John's ears perked up. Rarely did she mention Holly in the years since she left, except in anger.

"When you got married," Clara said, "I thought she was taking from me the only person in the world I cared about." She took a deep breath. "Is it too late, John? Do you think you might be able to find Holly?"

John cast her a sharp look. Only that morning, when Skelly Wilks came for John's milk, he brought a note from Dixie at the Do-Drop Inn. He wondered if Clara knew. "I think I might find her," John said.

A sad smile creased Clara's lips as she nodded her approval. "I need you to hug me, son." John spread his arms, and Clara stepped into them. "I love you, John," she cried.

"I love you too, Mama."

Stranger with a wooden leg

John left for town an hour ago. It was well after dark when Clara finished putting away his clean laundry. She folded his shirts and underwear, and made sure his socks matched before she placed them in his chest drawer.

"Hello in there."

What was that? Clara jerked her head about, startled by what sounded like someone calling from outside the house.

She was reminded of the times in her childhood when the family was awakened by a man's deep voice calling from the front door. They had no phone when she was growing up, and the mail was too slow. Once every year or two a relative would show up from miles away without letting anybody know he was coming.

"Sam. Oh, Sam!" the voice would call, shattering the silence between midnight and dawn. Responding to the call, Clara's father recognized the voice. He'd crawl out of bed, and feel his way through the dark house to the front door. At the door, he stood face-to-face with a brother, a nephew, or a cousin he hadn't seen for years.

"Howdy, Sam."

"Come on in, Howard," her father said to his younger brother. "We'll find a place for you."

All the beds were full of kids.

Clara's mother got up and spread a pallet on the front room floor for the visitor to sleep on. Or sometimes her father transferred a kid to the pallet so the newcomer could have the bed the child was sleeping on.

Clara's Uncle Howard was a chain-smoking Baptist preacher who showed up every few years, each time with a new wife. Four times in all. But Uncle Howard died years ago, so Clara knew it wasn't the wandering minstrel calling from outside her door.

All her brothers and sisters were gone, except for her youngest brother Ned, and she had no idea where he was. The last time she saw him, Ned stopped by from wherever he came from on his way to wherever his wanderings were taking him. He pleaded with his older sister for money "to get him by" till he got on his feet again.

She didn't give him any money, so she was pretty sure it wasn't Ned's voice she heard outside her door. She hadn't seen nor heard from him since. Of the few relatives left that she remembered, she wasn't close enough with any of them for them to pay her an unannounced visit.

"Hello in there!"

She listened hard. The voice sounded like—No, it couldn't be. A bit irritated at the intrusion, she wondered why whoever he was didn't knock on the door.

"Anybody home?"

Clara opened the door and peered into the darkness. She saw no one. She flipped on the porch light, and—At the bottom of the steps stood a white-haired man with a neatly trimmed beard and a broad grin.

"Hello, Clara."

What in the name of heaven! She hadn't heard the voice for many years, but she knew who it belonged to.

"Kyle?"

"My my, aren't you the pretty one?" he said.

Dumbfounded, Clara opened her mouth, but couldn't think of anything to say. Finally locating her voice, she said, "What are you doing here?"

"Waiting for you to invite me in."

"Well, you— It's been a long time."

"Much too long, Clara." His eyes grew misty. "I'll make it up to you, if you'll give me time."

With an obvious effort, he climbed the steps to the porch, favoring his left leg.

Kyle stopped by the Sak 'n Pak Store, wondering if Simon Colby was still there. He was not surprised that he was. Kyle reminded Simon of who he was, since Simon hadn't recognize the beard, the mustache, and the full head of white hair. He asked Simon about Clara and John, and was pleased to learn they were still on the farm.

Kyle was uneasy about showing up at the farm without giving notice. He was afraid Clara wouldn't want anything to do with him after all those years. To himself he confessed, as he had many times since the day he disappeared, it wasn't fair to her and John to leave the way he did. He didn't mean to be gone forever, but the longer he waited to come back, the easier it became to stay away.

The days grew into months, and the months into years. Too many years.

"Go home, Kyle," Simon told him. "If she don't want you back, it won't take long to find out, and you won't be any worse off than you are now. If she wants you, you've hit the mother lode."

With the pale blue eyes Clara remembered, still sharp in his advanced age, Kyle appraised the woman he always loved but had trouble living with. Even so, he took the chance of returning to be with her and their son, though they might not want him back.

"Are you going to ask me in?"

Into her kitchen Clara invited total strangers who knocked on her back door for coffee in the dead of winter, or for a cold drink in the heat of summer. But, seeing this man, whom she neither seen nor heard from for nearly thirty years, the man who went away one day without saying goodbye, and who had shown up on her front porch on a hot summer night without telling her he was coming—Clara was shocked into near paralysis.

She stared at him. The beard, the mustache, the flashing smile, the old blue eyes still sparkled. Tall, slightly stooped, but agile for his age. This was Kyle Willingham, the man she married, the father of her son, the man she lived with for eleven years, and lived without for going on thirty. And now, there he stood, looking her squarely in the face with a patient grin, waiting for her answer, wondering whether he hit the mother lode. Was she going to invite him in as he hoped, or would she tell him to go back to the same hell he survived? Clara felt herself pushing the door open, stepping aside to let Kyle hobble past.

Once inside, he paused, and glanced about, recalling what the room looked like when he last saw it. With a solemn nod, he was satisfied not much changed.

Clara waved him to the sofa.

"Tell me about John," Kyle said.

She was surprised at the abrupt question. "John? John lives here. He's gone into town. He'll be back soon."

This time John told her where he was going, why he was going, and when he would be back. He was going to bring Holly home.

"He's living here—with you?" Kyle asked. "Is he not married?"

She hesitated for less than a split second. "Oh, yes," she said, satisfied that her response answered both questions.

"Do we have grand kids?"

"Not yet."

He didn't need to know about Holly's miscarriages.

Kyle nodded, having expected a bit more.

"Why are you hobbling around so?" Clara asked.

He patted his left leg, sticking out straight and stiff as a board. "A souvenir from the Kumwha Valley."

"The Kumwha Valley?"

"Korea, 1952."

Korea? Clara was shocked. John was in Korea.

"They tried a while to save it," Kyle said, "but I finally told them to cut it off and give me a new leg. It's fifteen years old now, not as pretty as the original," he said with a mischievous grin, "but it works." The grin faded. "Most everything works if you give it time enough, Clara"

"Do you want to tell me about it?"

"Not yet," he said. "There'll be time."

"Are you well?"

"Fit as a fiddle." Chuckling, he said, "A one-legged fiddle. How about you?"

"I'm all right." This was not the time to tell him about Josie's death and John's trial. Kyle didn't know who Holly was, so there was no need talking about her. Maybe she wouldn't have to tell him Holly hadn't been there for three years. Not yet anyway.

"What has happened to you all these years?" she said. "You know John will want to know."

"Yes, I know. It's a long story, Clara. A very long story. Two wars, bumming around. Odds and ends of life that came together the day I worked up the nerve to come home. Maybe one day there'll be time to tell you about it."

"How much of it don't you want me to know?"

"Not much. But can I choose the time to tell you?"

Though Clara wasn't ready to reveal her secrets, Kyle knew the time would come when he'd have tell her his, especially if she allowed him to stay around, which was not yet settled.

One day he'd have to tell her about the time he spent harvesting wheat in Kansas and Nebraska, riding corn planters in Iowa and Illinois. Repairing houses in the ghettos of Baltimore. Sweeping the streets and shoveling snow in Chicago. And the wars.

He'd tell her of the weeks and months after he left, of wandering with a troubled mind from place to place, looking for a reason to stop. He found it after Pearl Harbor. He joined the army, and survived the slaughter of Normandy Beach.

He'd tell her about being called back to service in '52 when the Chinese swarmed across the Korean border, about the mortar barrage in the Kumwha Valley that shattered his leg. The shell exploded in the midst of a gun crew, leaving seven U. S. soldiers dead, and the eighth man who thought he was. The Chinese thought so too. When the medic got there, he checked the lone survivor's dog tag. The name on it said he was Kyle Willingham. That was when Kyle promised himself, "If I get out of this alive, I'm going home."

Sometime when the ground was white with snow, and the fireplace in the living room ablaze, savoring one of Clara's sweet rolls and coffee, he'd tell her of the months of recovery from surgery, about the doctors' efforts to save the leg, and telling them to "cut that sucker off and let me out of here."

The part he would put off to the last, because it would be the most painful to talk about, was a young nurse named Risa who stayed by him through the surgery, during the long period of recovery and rehab, who took him in and cared for him after the hospital told him they could do no more for him. Risa suffered with him while he struggled with laborious effort and determination to walk again, finally on a wooden stick where there once was a leg.

Some day he'd tell Clara all of it, including the part about falling in love with Risa though she was several years younger than he, how he suffered with her as her body faded away, decimated by cancer.

But the time was not now. And he wondered, when the time came, would it have been long enough to ease the pain? For whom? Clara? Or himself?

"You thought you'd just stroll back here, show up at my front door," Clara said, "take up where you left off, and thirty years of being gone would just fade away. Was that it?"

"Well, I'll tell you, Clara—"

"You know, of course, I'm not the one you hurt most by taking off without saying anything to anybody."

Kyle studied the floor around the stub of a leg.

"I know," he said, "and I'm not—"

"John has lived with it for all these years. It took some time for me, but I finally got used to your not being beside me when I woke up in the morning. It cut deep for John."

"I—I truly regret that. I never meant to hurt anybody. And I've lived with it every night and every day the whole time."

"Now I guess you've come home to die," Clara said, not spitefully, but with an edge to her words.

"No, Clara."

He took a moment to line up the words he wanted to say, something to help her understand.

"I've been dying for thirty years," he said, "ever since I drove away that day and didn't come back. "Not a day passed when I didn't want to turn around and come back, but I was afraid. Afraid you wouldn't let me in, and there was no way I could blame you for that. "Come home to die, Clara? No, I've come home to live."

He smiled then, a mischievous smile. "It

occurred to me—one of these mornings I'm going to wake up old, and I didn't want to be by myself when it happened."

She stared at him with a steady gaze, trying to figure out what was in his mind. She confessed to John that she was unfair to his father. Honesty would tell her she needed Kyle now more than ever. She always missed him, but there were times in the still of late nights when she hated him for going away.

Now, John was gone to bring Holly home, depriving her of more time with John. Without Kyle she would be alone again. But how long would it take for things to be the way they were before Kyle left? Could they ever be the same? Or would life be better with Kyle now, with the changes people go through, especially older people for whom aloneness was sometimes fatal?

But thirty years! Where did they go? How much of life went with them? And how much of it was left? Did she want to spend whatever time remained of her life with Kyle Willingham? What could she do? After all, Kyle did come home.

Maybe what he brought with him was what she needed to help survive the uncertainty she anticipated with Holly's return. Could she just boot Kyle out the door he came in through, and slam it on his back as he left? And what about John? How would he react to Kyle's limping back hale and hardy, even with half a leg on the left side, ready to be his father again? Time alone would tell.

Finally, "buck up and make the most of it," made its way to the front of her thinking. Give old wounds time to heal. "You devil," she said with a grin. "You're already old."

"But not as old as I'm going to be."

She gave that a pensive nod. "I'll put the pot on." Half way to the kitchen, she said, "You still like it black?"

"Yes, ma'am. Hot and black." He pondered whether he had struck what Simon called the mother lode.

Reunion

John focused his eyes on the neon sign above the door of Dixie's Do-Drop Inn. Dixie's note said she would be there. His heart was pounding like it might explode out of his plaid shirt. He couldn't wait to get close to her, and yet he was afraid their meeting after three years might not go right. What if she were different now from before? Maybe she married again, and hadn't come alone. If so, he had no interest in meeting her new husband.

No matter. He had to see her, and find out for himself why she decided to come back, and maybe why she left. Flooding back came the memories of the good times he and Holly shared, along with bewilderment of why she left without telling where she was going. Just like his father. He wondered if the time would ever come when he'd have a chance to find out about him. Why he left. Where he was, and what he did while he was gone.

Half a block away, John saw a slender young woman. She pushed open the glass front door to Dixie's and went inside.

That night after Holly left he stood for a long

time, staring at the bed in the upstairs room where he and she slept, feasting his eyes on everything she touched. Looking for some way to reach out to her, to connect with her wherever she was, by some magical quirk of fate he might bring her back. Something to tell him where she was, so he could go and bring her home.

The Rinso white sheets, the fluffy pillows, the bed spread she was so proud of making. Her fluffy little blue house slippers parked with the toes sticking out from under the bed. The dresses, the tops and bottoms, jeans and jackets that filled the closet she called hers. Everything of hers he left where it was the day she went away. What she left behind hurt almost as much as what she took with her. Facing the reality of her leaving, even so, John never lost hope that one day she'd find her way back.

And now, there she was.

The sadness that hovered over him like that little dark cloud wherever he went, the longing, the wondering where she was and what happened to her. He could put it all behind him now.

It was her all right. The years didn't dim his memory of her walking, narrow shoulders leaning slightly forward, her head leading the way, as though every step was carefully planned before she took it.

John moved with anxious steps toward Dixie's.

He pushed the door open and stepped inside. He saw her sitting at the counter, sipping at a cup of coffee. With cream and a spoonful of sugar, he remembered. Slight of build, her blond head covered with a white scarf.

Dixie was standing behind the counter, her eyes glued to the door, as though anticipating John's arrival. She breathed a deep sigh when John came through the door, relieved, half afraid he wouldn't come.

She caught John's eye with a slight nod in Holly's direction. He didn't have to be told the woman at the counter with her back to him was the one he came to take home, hoping she'd want to go with him.

Three stools to her right, Boomer Blacklage's belly hung over his belt, nudging the counter. He saw John ease over and sit down on the chrome stool next to the woman with hazel, gold-flecked eyes, wearing dark glasses.

Boomer loaded his fork with hotcake dripping with Aunt Jemima's. He maneuvered the fork into his mouth with a don't-bother-me-when-I'm-eating shake of his frowzy head. But when John sat down beside the lady at the counter, Boomer stopped eating long to take a look.

Boomer knew who John was, not sure about the lady in the dark glasses.

Goober McCracken was a loafer by trade. He practiced loafing for so long and so diligently he developed it into an art form.

Nobody in the county could loaf longer nor better than Goober. Other people stopped entering County Fair loafing contests because they knew they couldn't out loaf Goober. He even contacted the Guinness people to see if they would put him in their book of records. They said they'd think about it. That was six years ago. They were still thinking.

Goober was in the middle of sopping one of Dixie's home-made buttermilk biscuits in what was left of a country fried steak and mashed potatoes drowned in white gravy. When John came through the door, the biscuit was half way to Goober's mouth. It stuck there while he watched John park his backside on the stool beside the lady at the counter.

Few people in Blessing remembered the last time they went to Dixie's when Bubba Whitstone was not playing the pinball machine by the front door. Once Bubba homed in on the flashing lights, the bells, and the ricocheting silver balls, reality took flight.

But even Bubba looked up when he heard John say, "Hello, Holly."

She must have known he'd come.

John wondered why she didn't call him at the farm instead of calling Dixie. He guessed it was because she knew Clara would pick up the phone, and she wasn't yet ready for conversation with her ex-mother-in-law.

"Hello, John," Holly said, with that husky voice, memories of which disturbed John's sleep.

Her long-fingered artist's hands were wrapped around the coffee cup. She was three years older, her features somewhat drawn, but time didn't diminish her perfect complexion and provocative mouth.

"I've missed you," John said.

Dixie placed a cup on the counter in front of him, poured it full, and refilled Holly's cup.

"For a while," Holly said, "I hoped you'd come looking for me."

"I did. I drove all night in the direction Susan said the bus went. But I didn't know—"

"Of course, you had no idea where I was, and I didn't want to call the farm. I'm sorry, John. I shouldn't have done you that way." She covered his hand with hers. "Your mother and I didn't get along well, but I've had time to understand her side too now."

"I never thought you'd stay gone."

"I didn't think so either, but after the divorce—"

"You got a divorce?"

"I was afraid you wouldn't take me back. Then at a restaurant I met this guy named Frank Crother. He was an over-the-road trucker. Sometimes he was gone for weeks at a time. He drank a lot, and it got so I couldn't wait for him to leave, hoping he would never come back. "One day he didn't. Three months ago he ran off the road some place in Ohio. The tractor flipped and burned. They said there wasn't enough left of Frank to bury."

She removed the head scarf and shook her hair loose. It fell to her shoulders. "I was the only one who was married," she said. "Frank never was."

She rummaged in her purse for something she couldn't find. "Do you have a cigarette, John?"

He took the pack of Camels from his shirt pocket and shook one out. "I never knew you to smoke," he said.

"I never did before."

He struck a match. Holly held the cigarette to

the flame, and exhaled a cloud of smoke.

"Frank was the kind of man who brought out the worst in people," she said.

"Why did you stay?"

"I've asked myself that question a thousand times. I guess it was because Frank was good to me when he was sober, which was not often. Or maybe it was because I blew one marriage and didn't want it to happen again. Women do strange things sometimes, John. We start thinking maybe the rough stuff is our fault. We stay, hoping things will get better."

She blew out a cloud of smoke. "It took a long time for me to realize that a man doesn't change just because you want him to, or because he says he will. After a while, you know he's not going to, but by then you feel like you're tarnished merchandise, afraid nobody else would want you. That's the trap."

"What brought you back?"

"You did," Holly said. "I never stopped loving you, but I didn't know whether you found someone else. After Frank was killed I made up my mind I was coming back no matter what happened."

"You and Mama—it wasn't your fault, Holly."

"It's hard for two women to live in the same house. It was your mother's house, and I was the intruder."

"It's different now. Mama's different. She wants you back."

She squeezed his hand. "Oh, John, I love you so much."

"Do you want to go home?" he asked? "I told Mama I'd bring you back with me."

She crushed the cigarette in a glass ashtray. "Yes," she said. "You don't know how good that sounds."

"Let's go." He took her hand and led her away with an arm across her shoulders.

Boomer snarfed his hotcakes, Bubba pounded the pinball machine, and Goober swabbed his plate with the buttermilk biscuit.

Life at Dixie's Do Drop Inn returned to normal.

Homecoming

Clara and Holly didn't hesitate. They greeted each other with forgiving embraces as only two women can. Hugs can cancels past sins, and open the door to better times to come. Clara introduced Kyle as "John's father," then led Holly away to the kitchen with an arm across her shoulders.

John's reunion with his father was tentative. To John, he was looking at the face of a stranger, old, wrinkled, gray. Stooped. Half a leg on the left side.

What became of the man who was once his father? Over the years the image of the father, with whom he had such fun as a young boy, faded. Was this the same man for whom he shed painful tears, whose face became a blur with time, scarcely recognizable?

At first, John's acceptance of his father's return was probationary. He put Kyle on trial, giving himself time to decide whether this was the man he wanted to call dad. Over cups of Clara's coffee, they traded experiences from Korea, sparring a bit at times, seeking common ground, where reconciliation slowly melded into renewed respect for who they were. Father and son.

They toured the fields of corn, milo, and soybeans aboard the Allis Chalmers tractor. John drove, and Kyle did most of the talking. In the end, they made unspoken agreement to put the past behind them. They laughed and cried and hugged, and made plans for the time they had left together.

Unsolved remains the mystery of what prompted Dudley Coe to interrupt court proceedings to confess a crime of which no one believed him capable. Speculation was he had little to look forward to in life since his son Wesley died, and Sara Jo left him.

Maybe Dudley's muddled mind told him by basking for a moment in the sunlight of notoriety, relieving his mind of a burden of guilt, he could make amends for an aimless life. Who could perceive the inner workings of a dejected mind at a given moment?

Dudley's confession cost him his life at the hands of a hothead with less than a week to serve for a minor offense. Under the nails of Luther Gaston were discovered particles of blood that led to his conviction for the murder of Dudley Coe. June 7, 1969, Gaston was put to death in the Oklahoma State Prison.

His body was never claimed.

Will Starkey knew well to where his ill-advised attack of a witness could lead. Contempt of court would be the least painful charge. More serious was the possibility he could be suspended. Or he could be disbarred, have his license revoked, and never again be allowed to practice law.

Much depended on the judge's view of the incident. Starkey tried to convince himself, legal ethics aside, even Judge Yokum couldn't deny that Coe deserved the smack across the mouth for his contemptuous testimony. Still, Starkey was a veteran lawyer with the rules of conduct emblazoned on his brain, and he couldn't excuse himself for having attacked a witness.

Starkey became the subject of an extensive investigation. The Chief Disciplinary Counsel and the Regional Disciplinary Committee of the state of Oklahoma agreed he be reprimanded for unethical conduct, and suspended his license for one year.

Starkey was relieved. He was still a lawyer, and could practice again after only twelve months. Starkey spent his suspension as a clerk in the law offices of Charlie Bates. The day the state Supreme Court granted the reinstatement of Starkey's license, Bates asked him if he'd like to be a partner in his law firm.

Starkey said yes.

Simon Colby promised himself if he ever got to be eighty years old he'd throw the lock on the door of the Sak 'n Pak Store and walk away from it. That's what he did. Three months later he suffered a stroke. Doc Sloan put him in the nursing home in Blessing.

Skelly Wilks brought Simon a fresh pot of black coffee every morning until Simon died at age eighty-one. Seth Gibbs buried Simon beside Thelma in the Baptist Church cemetery.

Prudence "Limpy" Logan was relieved of his duties as "the sheriff" of Blessing. Limpy was not upset. All the deputy's job did was interfere with his fishing and hunting. And besides, he was rankled that he never received the raise in pay Arthur Hicks promised.

Even so, with all that behind him, Limpy could sleep now without interruption. No longer would he be harassed by the commanding voice of Louise Whitworth. He, in fact, instructed Louise never to disturb him for any reason except for her funeral.

A month later, Louise applied for, and was granted, her old job back at what she called the funny farm.

Dude Martin found Hamp Hargove's body on his front room floor. The walls and ceiling were splattered with blood. The muzzle of a shotgun was pointed where his chin once was.

Martin came to tell Hamp the farmers agreed to sell out to the Arkansas hog outfit.

ABOUT THE AUTHOR

An accomplished author with many books to his credit, David A. Estes draws on his wide experience, from the cotton fields of Oklahoma and Texas where he grew up, to the islands of the South Pacific where he served as a United States Marine, to the market place in America where he retired from a career in broadcasting.

David writes westerns and mysteries, along with many other genres of novels and short stories. He lives on his family farm in West Central Missouri with two black Labs and a suspicious cat.

OTHER PUBLICATIONS BY DAVID A. ESTES

Available at amazon.com, barnsandnoble.com, abebooks.com and more

Angel on My Back
Wet Dogs Don't Ride
Blood on the Wall
A Bag of Gold

Coming Soon:
Ajax and Elbow Grease
Big Boy